On the Back
of the Beast

S F Chapman

Striped
Cat
Press

www.stripedcatpress.com

On the Back of the Beast
by
S F Chapman
is also available
as a Kindle e-Book

Learn more about the author at www.SFChapman.com

The pawing cat logo is a trademark of
Striped Cat Press.

Cover by Anderson Solutions and Design
Anderson_solutions_design@yahoo.com

Striped Cat Press
First Paperback Edition, Third Printing:
August 2013

To Richard "Tino" Remillard,
a recently departed brother-in-law
and good friend.
His industrious nature has been
the inspiration for many
of my characters over the years.

Acknowledgements

This question comes up with great regularity when I discuss my novels with readers: Is it difficult to write about situations where your characters are put in peril?

The answer is no. If it is exciting and perhaps a bit scary to read, it was *so* exciting and scary to write.

On the Back of the Beast was certainly an exhilarating effort for me.

I had some great help with the book. Thank you to my teenage daughter Tina, who helped me to create and name many of the characters. My son David helped me brainstorm various places where you *wouldn't* want to be in a major earthquake. Thanks also to my longtime friends Betty, Charles and Victoria. The characters Flint and Reesa are modeled after Charles and Betty. Their teenage daughter Victoria provided much of the plucky can-do attitude that inspired the creation of Gwen.

I'd like to thank my three excellent editors: Mark, Clinton and Christina. Clint was also the inspiration for his namesake: Cat Torres's Jaguar mechanic.

The Second Grade teacher, Mrs. Cunningham, is largely based on my longtime pal, Nancy Lane, who teaches at The Seven Hills School in Walnut Creek, California. Nancy allowed me to help out in her classroom for many weeks as I wrote *On the Back of the Beast*. She described to me surviving a huge earthquake as a Kindergartner in the late 1970's. I borrowed from her story when I wrote about Gwen's narrow escape from the classroom at Lincoln Grade School.

Thank you.

Introduction

I have lived my entire life in the San Francisco Bay Area. It is a wonderful seven thousand or so square miles of both natural beauty and man-made creations wrapped around a huge bluish-gray estuary that spills into the Pacific at the Golden Gate.

The Bay Area is America's 5th largest metropolitan area and the Hayward Fault slices from north to south right through the center of it.

Unlike the more famous and jittery San Andreas Fault to the west that destroyed San Francisco in 1906, the lesser-known Hayward Fault has remained ominously dormant for over 140 years. Earthquake faults do not sleep forever.

When the rather moderate Loma Prieta Earthquake struck south of the San Francisco Bay Area in 1989, I became fascinated with the sense of communal denial that blinds the residents of Northern California to the omnipresent danger. A *huge* seismic disaster is inevitable.

Nearly everyone who has survived a major earthquake can tell a tale with razor sharpness of their particular situation when the ground moved. Many people admit to doing exactly the wrong things at that moment: working high up on a ladder, gazing out of a skyscraper window, rummaging around in the basement of a brick building, landing a crowded jumbo jet.

I strove to capture these sorts of survivor's stories when I wrote *On The Back Of The Beast.*

1. A particularly splendid morning

"*Dad*; we're gonna be late again," Kayla sullenly noted as she slumped forward on the well-worn bench seat of the ancient Ford truck.

Gary Hendley pressed the horn and the idling pickup bellowed a second time.

The lacy window curtains of the neighbor's unlit house parted. An old woman peered out into early morning gloom for the source of the disturbance.

"I'll get kicked out of English tutoring if I'm late again," Kayla groaned. The seventeen-year-old thrust aside an avalanche of rumpled chestnut hair from her puffy and pockmarked face.

"My life sucks," she pouted.

Gary's eyes narrowed as he stared at the front door of his brother-in-law's house, "I'm not too happy about this either, but I told your Uncle Doug that I'd give him a ride to the BART Station this morning." The wiry forty-two year-old carpenter glanced at his wristwatch: 6:07 AM. "DAMN IT! Kayla, jump out and ring his doorbell. Hopefully he's not still in bed."

The teenager reluctantly pulled at the passenger door lever.

On the Back of the Beast

The porch light of the little house blinked on as the front door opened. Doug Hunter waved to the impatient occupants of the truck before he stepped out and locked up.

He trotted to the waiting vehicle and scooted in next to Kayla. "Sorry about the delay. I was on the toilet when you drove up."

Gary depressed the clutch, shifted into first gear and directed the pickup down the dark street. "We can't keep driving you around, Doug."

"Yeah; I know," the scruffy roustabout buckled his seat belt, "I'm gonna pick up a new radiator for my crappy old car after work. I'll put it in tonight and everything should be good for tomorrow." Doug poked at his morose niece, "What's the good news, Kayla?"

The girl scowled.

Gary answered for his grumpy daughter; "She hates high school and is sure they're going to kick her out soon."

"She wouldn't be the first one in this family," Doug noted.

The truck pulled into the parking lot of the train station and Doug jumped out. "Thanks for the ride." He closed the squeaky door and bustled off to catch the 6:25 train to Berkeley.

Gary turned left onto California Street and drove towards Jefferson High School.

• • •

Ida Martinez warily looked up and down the nearly deserted Fruitvale District street before she pulled the key for the front door of the tiny old market from her pocket.

The tattered and gray shopkeeper had grown especially leery about the neighborhood during the dozen years since her cherished husband was shot to death in the store during a robbery.

She twisted the key, slipped through the barely opened door and switched on the lights. Manny's Market was now open for business.

Ida shuffled to the checkout counter. On the wall behind the decrepit mechanical cash register was a small silver-framed black and white photo of a smiling Hispanic gentleman. She sighed; it was her favorite picture of Manny. Ida kissed her index finger and gently caressed the photo of her beloved spouse. Her finger slipped down to the small gash that pierced the wall just below the photograph.

The bullet that had killed him had made the hole.

She traced the ragged edges of the laceration. Her son Jim had wanted to patch the damaged wallboard before they reopened the market after the murder, but Ida insisted that it should remain as a grisly reminder of how fast a life can be destroyed.

The old woman tilted her head in sorrow as she studied the little memorial. With the gangs, prostitutes and shootings, the community was in a steep decline. She and Jim could just barely afford to keep the little market open.

Ida hobbled to the small iron safe bolted securely to the floor behind cigarette case. She withdrew the sparsely-filled money drawer and inserted it into the cash register. Ida hoisted herself onto the wooden stool behind the worn counter and turned on the old desk radio for company.

The receiver crackled to life, "...*It's going to be a particularly splendid October morning in the San Francisco Bay Area. The Mighty AM 600 forecast calls for our warm and windy fall weather to continue, the highs will be in the mid 70's in most areas and the lows in the mid 60's...*"

• • •

Four thousand miles to the southwest, high above the Pacific Ocean, Captain Burt Weaver stared pensively out of the cockpit window of the immense passenger plane. Long ago as a Naval aircraft carrier-based cargo pilot, he had developed the habit of scanning the vastness of the sea for anomalies. More than once, far off near the horizon, he'd seen peculiarities. Sometimes it was just whales, occasionally freighters and once he spotted a huge Soviet sub.

"Captain;" the First Officer repeated his observation, "we're going to have a low fuel warning again by the time we reach San Francisco."

"I hate it when they do this to us," he mumbled. Burt straightened up in the pilot's seat and adjusted the navy blue buttons on his polyester flight crew jacket. "Alright, let the company know first, then SFO." He winced and added, "Tell air traffic that I want to come straight in, no holding pattern while they get their crap together."

"Yes sir."

Burt Weaver returned to his reflective scrutiny of the dark ocean far below. It was considered quite an honor to pilot the newest jets for a carrier as large as Pacifica Airlines.

He knew that one of the few reasons that Pacifica had stayed profitable enough to buy this plane during the recent recession was due to the Accounting Department program called *Maximum Capacity/ Maximum Profits*. Burt stroked his perfectly trimmed white mustache, almost everyone in the company just called it "stuffing." It came down to this, no Pacifica plane ever left the gate without being stuffed to the maximum take-off weight with the minimum fuel load to safely complete the flight.

Burt ruminated that the unending argument between the pilot's union and management centered on what exactly was the minimum fuel load to safely complete a flight.

Captain Weaver glanced forward; far to the east he could see the first faint light of dawn.

• • •

"Rowan! COME ON!" Gwen Mills tersely tugged on her little brother's wrist as he dithered his way past the busy First and Second Grade playground, "Mom told me to take you *straight* to Kindergarten!"

The distracted boy turned to his eight-year-old sister. "But I wanna play here!" he implored.

"You can't! This playground isn't for little kids." Gwen made her sternest face, "Kindergartners have to use the Preschool playground. Now come on!"

With one hand clamped tightly around Rowan's thin wrist, Gwen Mills pulled open the door of

6

the shabby Kindergarten room. She pushed her reluctant brother into the pandemonium of the crowded classroom.

The girl watched her brother scamper off to the Arts and Crafts table.

With her required task completed, Gwen gleefully skipped off to enjoy a few minutes of play before class began. She ran her fingers along the walls of the "C" Wing classrooms as she passed by. There were four second grade rooms in the wing and her class, C-1, was directly in front of the towering new play structure. She stepped into the tan bark filled arena of the First and Second Grade Play Area.

Good; she grinned, no one was on the Monkey Bars.

Gwen climbed onto the low wooden platform and stepped to the edge. Just above her head was the wavy red framework of rungs that made up the Monkey Bars. Below was the freshly laid bark that still smelled like pine trees. Most kids pretended that the bark below the Monkey Bars was burning hot lava. Gwen liked to imagine that the lumpy brown mass was really a dark African river that hid hungry crocodiles that waited for foolish little monkeys high above to misjudge the distance between tree branches as they swung playfully through the air.

On the Back of the Beast

She gazed up at the first bar, raised her hands in front of her and made a colossal leap. Gwen grasped the first rung and swung forward to skip the second and reach directly for the third red bar.

"*Gwen Mills!*" a deep male voice boomed, "You know better than that!"

She hung there on the third bar and twisted towards the adult who supervised the play yard. It was Mr. Newman, the imposing new Fourth Grade teacher. He waved for her to come to him. Gwen sighed as she dropped down to the bark river; another poor little monkey would be eaten by the fearsome crocodiles.

Gwen trudged to the beckoning teacher, "Yes, Mr. Newman?"

The tall man tilted his head and smiled pleasantly, "Gwen, are we allowed to skip rungs on the Monkey Bars?" His black eyebrows arched up expectantly.

"No, Mr. Newman."

He reached down and tousled her brown hair, "I know it's easy for a talented Second Grader like you to skip bars, but most of the little First Graders who try it fall and get hurt." He set his big hand on her slumped shoulders, "We all need to set a good example for the little kids."

8

Gwen nodded ruefully.

With a wide grin he added, "You still have a few minutes to play before the bell rings."

The little girl swiveled around and ran off.

2. The Mighty AM 600

Lloyd Gozport is a genius, Frank Johnson thought as he idly looked though the project summary in the subdued coffee house. Probably an evil genius, he mused sardonically.

The rugged Electrical Engineer carefully studied the history of the job site. The up-and-coming San Francisco media mogul Lloyd Gozport, soon to be his new boss, had bought the prime mountain top transmitter site of a failed Christian AM radio station for only thirty thousand dollars. Lloyd had spent one and a half million last summer for a huge new antenna and state of the art automated transmitter. Now he charged fifty thousand dollars a month to broadcast the signal from a Modesto radio station. Apparently he would make a huge profit on his tiny investment in just over two years.

Frank sipped his black coffee as the slumberous regulars wandered in for their required morning beverage. Frank checked his watch: 6:37 AM. His cohorts were late.

Officially Frank had retired about three years ago from Delta/Wye Power Systems, but the leisurely life of a retiree did not suit him. After driving his wife and friends batty for months, he finally decided to open a small consulting firm.

Frank chuckled; *small* meant he worked alone in his basement in Louisville, Colorado. He had taken on several minor jobs and then Lloyd Gozport called him two weeks ago with this giant new project.

He flew to the Bay Area last night for today's site assessment. Gozport wanted to expand the mountain top site by adding two new FM transmitters and possibly a TV station transmitter. All that new hardware on the top of the remote Bay Area mountain would require a vast amount of dependable electrical power and that was Frank's specialty.

The friendly little jingle of Frank's cell phone interrupted the serene sleepiness of the café, "Hello? Yes, this is Frank Johnson. I'm at the coffee shop on Clayton Road."

"OK, I'll meet you in the parking lot in five minutes. I just have a rental car. Should I follow you up to the mountain top?"

Frank balked at the reply, "Yeah; I guess we can all squeeze into your SUV. Five minutes, right. I'll see you then, bye."

Frank drained the last of the now-cold coffee, gathered up the project summary and stepped out into the blustery morning air.

• • •

On the Back of the Beast

Catalina Torres glanced at the wall mirror next to the door of the turquoise painted mudroom.

She looked excellent, as always, she decided.

The tall and smartly-dressed dark-haired woman grinned at her reflection. She retrieved the architectural drawings from the side table, pushed open the ornate wooden door and briskly walked across the alleyway to the enormous garage of her equally enormous house. A smug little grin crept across her face. These gaudy indulgences were the rewards for talent, hard work and a huge amount of good luck.

Cat, as nearly everyone called her, stepped into the long narrow building that contained her collection of a dozen high performance cars. Today would hopefully be a Jaguar day, she thought as she bypassed the shiny blue MG and the vintage Corvette.

Her hand brushed across the back of the red XKE. She smiled; the hood of the vehicle was closed. In a long ago agreed upon signal, her mechanic had finally finished repairing the temperamental English roadster and closed the hood of the sports car.

Cat slipped into the ebony leather seat of her favorite car and laid the stout roll of house plans on the passenger seat. A grease-smudged note was propped between the chrome gear shifter and the console. She retrieved the scrawly message from her tireless mechanic, *Cat --- Take it easy. I just replaced two exhaust valves. They still stick sometimes. Enjoy, Clint.*

The sleek red roadster roared to life. Cat spent a patient five minutes idling to warm up the finicky triple carburetor engine. This little jaunt through the twists and turns of the Oakland Hills would be an especially good trip to take in the twitchy English car. Cat activated the garage door opener and slowly backed the motorcar into the alleyway.

Her housekeeper plodded grimly down the long driveway. Cat slipped the Jaguar into neutral and waited for the woman.

After a pampered upbringing as the only child of renowned Northern California Hispanic Advertising Executive Emillo Torres and Catalonian Actress Cristina de Leon, Cat received a Masters in Fine Arts at the San Francisco Art Academy and seemed destined to follow her father into advertising. She instead surprised everyone by announcing that she would enter the School of Architecture at the University of California in Berkeley.

She immersed herself in her Architecture studies and often applied ideas from her Art School studies of form and sculpture to her early designs. Her huge home was only the most recent of Cat's grand architectural masterpieces.

She graduated in the top two percent of her class and took a well paying job at a large San Francisco architecture firm. But she soon became bored with the monotony of designing relatively conventional commercial buildings. With a substantial loan from her elderly parents, Cat opened her own firm on her thirtieth birthday.

Cat Torres Associates specialized in high-end and very innovative homes for the wealthy and adventurous. Cat's future was secured by her stunning design of the "Three Chessmen of the Apocalypse" house that she had created for her childhood friend, San Francisco musician Vince Flash. The unusual and controversial mansion, which resembled three giant chess pieces clustered together, was built high upon the hills that surrounded Santa Barbara. The house and its famous resident became an immediate tourist attraction.

Cat was deluged with requests for innovative design work. Today's little road trip was to straighten out some annoying construction details for a new mansion in the Oakland hills. She opened the window just as the housekeeper approached the vehicle, "Good Morning. I have to drop off these drawings. I'll be back at about eleven."

The housekeeper nodded and watched her boss zoom away in the snug red car. The vanity license plate on the back boasted, "CATZ CAR."

• • •

With one final painful jerk, the Jeep Cherokee careened from the steep and rutted gravel trail onto the freshly paved asphalt at the top of the mountain.

Tim O'Keefe eased his grip on the steering wheel and smiled in victory. He was officially called a "Transmitter Site Supervisor," but the spunky old Irishman had admitted to Frank that he was just one of Lloyd Gozport's underpaid lackeys.

"Here we are, Mr. Johnson. The transmitter site of the Mighty AM 600."

Frank Johnson flinched as he rubbed his throbbing right shoulder. The ride from the coffee shop to the gusty peak had taken about ninety minutes, but the last twenty minutes had been particularly frightening.

"Wow. Awesome view today!" Tim's twenty-seven year-old son TJ proclaimed from the backseat.

Tim circled the SUV around the new complex to show off the spectacular panorama of the East

Bay Area. "It's a bit hazy today but on a really clear day you can see the Farallon Islands to the west and the Sierra Nevada mountains to the east."

He parked the vehicle at the far edge of the pavement and the three men climbed out. "Lloyd told me to show you around and answer any questions. Where do you want to start?"

Frank studied the huge new steel broadcast tower that dominated the facility, the derelict wooden shack next to it with a much smaller red rusted antenna and the oversized white propane storage tank. He grinned and pointed towards the twin windowless gray cinder block structures at the far end of the asphalt, "What's in those buildings?"

"The one on the right has the transmitter and all of the electronics to keep the station running." The Irishman pointed to the other edifice, "That one there has the backup generator and the main electrical panel."

Frank nodded, "That's what I need to see."

Tim pulled a large jingly ring of keys from his pocket, "OK. Let's go take a look at them."

3. The subdued daily drudgery

Doug pulled his time card out of the middle of the metal rack and slid it into the slot of the time clock. 8:23 AM was officially embossed on the manila register.

He wandered to his workstation at Harmon Weld Shop and contemplated the jumble of charcoal gray angle iron parts that someone had piled on the pitted concrete floor next to the antiquated arc welder. Doug pulled the hand-written note from the control knob of the Lincoln stick welder. *SEE ME,* was all it said.

Doug rolled his eyes, wadded up the note and started the search through the compact labyrinth of the old brick building for his elusive employer.

• • •

From high up on the still unfinished roof of the gargantuan house, Gary Hendley paused with his framing hammer held in mid-stroke to watch the wind blow several wispy white plastic shopping bags around the heap of construction debris on the ground far below. He reminded himself to have the two day laborers load the discarded scraps into the yellow dumpster when they finished helping him on the roof.

On the Back of the Beast

Three weeks ago, work had largely stopped on the mansion while the owner, the architect and the building contractor argued over the framing details for the Sun Room. Most of the carpentry crew had been sent home or off to other projects until the difficulties could be resolved. But Gary was the lead carpenter on this job so he stayed behind to tend to the never-ending details that had to be worked out on a project of this size.

Luis waved to him, "OK, Boss. All done with nailing this part. Now what?"

Gary eyed the plywood stacked in the steep roof valley, "You and Alex need to nail those sheets to the hip rafters."

The dark and stocky man nodded. He turned to his much younger brother and bellowed the instructions in Spanish. The slim teenager leapt up and began dragging the panels to the proper location.

Gary chuckled as he watched the men. They'd been working here together off and on for weeks. Luis was about 30 years old and had lived in Bay Area for years. He spoke English well and was a better carpenter than some of the old Journeymen on the job. Alex looked like he was about 15 or 16 years old, spoke only Spanish and apparently had just moved to the area.

Gary smiled; Luis was constantly playing practical jokes on his gullible little brother.

Gary pounded the last of the nails flat. He twisted around to admire the dramatic view of the San Francisco Bay from the high vantage point of the building in the Oakland Hills. He could see four of the long and graceful bridges that arched across the broad harbor. In the distance, the office towers of San Francisco looked like fairy tale castles. Three silvery jets floated slowly in the distance as they lined up on the approach to San Francisco International Airport. Closer in, he could see the sparse office buildings of downtown Oakland and the monstrous stork-like cranes loading cargo at the busy port.

A short chirp from his phone announced a new text message. Gary withdrew the device from the pocket of his blue flannel shirt and studied the screen. *"The architect will deliver the revised plans this morning. Hopefully a full crew will work tomorrow..."*

• • •

Victor Mills climbed to the top of the huge stack of cargo containers above the deck of the *Kobe Meteor* docked at the sprawling Port of Oakland. It was almost 9 o'clock and they were supposed to have the *Kobe* loaded by ten. That wasn't going to happen. The dock supervisor had sent

19

him and Willy up on top to secure the load for departure.

"Hey Vick;" the burly Longshoreman joked as he joined the man, "did you sneak up here for a smoke?"

"Not today, Willy."

The two men stood together on the breezy tower of steel boxes. Willy pressed the two-way radio to his ear, "OK, we're in position. Send up the cables."

While they waited, the men talked. Willy gestured towards downtown Oakland, "Doesn't your wife work in one of those buildings?"

"Yeah," the slim man replied. "Over there. That tall ugly brown building to the left is Lisa's office. She's on the 12th floor. She tells me that she can see the Port from the break room." He shook his head mockingly, "But she can never figure out which ship I'm working on."

• • •

Lisa Mills slogged to her meager cubical. Her desk was piled high with work that had accumulated overnight at the incessantly busy insurance company. She straightened the mound of claims forms as she sat down. Her shoulders sagged and she kneaded her wrinkled brow. She was developing a horrid headache.

She restlessly fiddled with the mouse as she waited for the log-in screen to appear on the computer.

Lisa picked up the photo that perched on the edge of her desk: her little family. They were all standing together in the waves at the beach in Santa Cruz. Victor looked great, as always. Rowan was so little. Lisa grimaced; she looked so fat in this picture. Everyone wore sunglasses except Gwen. Lisa finally smiled; this was the photo that Gwen was sharing in her presentation today.

• • •

"Alright;" Mrs. Cunningham surveyed the group of nineteen jostling Second Graders circled around her on the floor, "next will be Nicholas."

The class groaned.

Gwen suppressed a giggle when the boy finally stood up and nearly tripped over Fiona. He stumbled his way to Mrs. Cunningham's side and stared at the rumpled paper that he held in front of his face.

Oh brother; Gwen thought, *what a dummy! They should have kept him in First Grade for another year.*

On the Back of the Beast

"Please begin, Nicholas," Mrs. Cunningham prompted the boy.

"My...name...is...Nicholas. I...am...seven," he labored. "I...am...in...Second Grade. I like...legos and...dinosaurs. My...sisters are Maddie and Kimmie and Mindy. My Dad works...at his work. I have...two uncles and...and two grandmas...and one grandpa." He smiled proudly.

With his two front teeth still missing, Gwen thought that he looked especially dopey.

The boy turned the sheet around and showed the assignment to his fidgety classmates. "This picture is Disneyland."

"This picture *was taken* at Disneyland," the teacher corrected.

"Yeah;" Nicholas nodded, "Disneyland."

Mrs. Cunningham sighed, "Thank you dear, you may sit down." She made a note in the grade book. "Gwen, I'd like for you to share your 'My Family' paper with us, please."

The effervescent brown-haired girl grinned at the mention of her name.

She walked to the place of honor and waved to her friends, Fiona and Isabelle. Gwen waited for her classmates to quiet down. She wanted their full attention for her presentation. When she had judged that they were ready, Gwen held her intricately decorated worksheet towards them for all to admire. Gwen had rehearsed for hours with her parents and would not need to read from the page.

"Good morning everyone. My name is Gwen Mills."

She paused and smiled to her peers, "I am eight years old and I am in Mrs. Cunningham's Second Grade class at Lincoln Grade School. My favorite things are playing on the Monkey Bars, reading, camping and kittens. My brother, Rowan, is in Ms Chin's Kindergarten class. He is five. My Mom works at United Insurance in Oakland, her name is Lisa Mills. My Dad's name is Victor. He's a Longshoreman and gets to work on giant ships. Sometimes he works all night. We don't have any pets and I don't have any Aunts, Uncles or Grandparents."

"No grandparents?" Jason interjected.

Gwen shrugged, "They all died a long time ago."

Mrs. Cunningham glared at the pudgy boy, "No more interruptions, Jason."

Gwen's hazel eyes gleamed as she pointed to the photograph that was carefully glued to the center of the worksheet, "This is a picture of my family that was taken at the beach in Santa Cruz."

"Very good, Gwen."

• • •

Kayla had struggled her way through English tutoring and first period Civics at Jefferson High School without major catastrophes. But now she was about to confront her most painful daily challenge: second period Remedial Elementary Mathematics. She stood at the door and her classmates filed past her. Kayla closed her eyes and lamented that this was a class for losers who couldn't handle real math and she wasn't even able to keep up.

She crept into the room and headed to her seat.

"Kayla."

She turned towards the large wooden teacher's deck next to the white board. Mr. Brown gestured to her and Kayla warily approached the man.

"This note was just dropped off," he examined the folded white message. "They want you to go down to the counseling office right now." The teacher winced as he silently finished reading the sheet. "Apparently, they want to move you to Harrison Alternative School."

He refolded the page and slipped it into his shirt pocket. "I know that you've been struggling with the material since the school year began," his voice trailed off when he realized that the teenager was weeping.

Kayla crumbled in defeat. A curtain of unruly hair cascaded forward to cover her anguished face.

She had failed again.

Now they wanted to send her to the school for misfits and underachievers. She whimpered uncontrollably as she plodded out of the Math room.

Mr. Brown watched the dejected girl leave his classroom with a sense of sad consternation, "Good luck, Kayla."

4. The period of portents

Kayla sobbed during most of the long slow walk to the Main Office. She pushed open the door with puffy red eyes and a runny nose. The receptionist looked up and pointed to the back of the hectic workplace.

The school secretary rose from her desk across from the Counseling Office, "Kayla Hendley? Hi. How are you, dear?"

Kayla's eyes teared up again.

The woman handed her several tissues, "If you would go in and sit down, a counselor will meet with you shortly. Apparently they're all dealing with some problem right now in the Girl's locker room."

The demoralized teenager opened the grimy wooden door and staggered to the shabby gray sofa. The heavy glass panels that made up the partition walls of the small office shuddered in disharmony when the door slammed shut.

Kayla collapsed on the sofa and wailed uncontrollably.

• • •

Doug grumbled to himself as he carried the order form and shop drawings back to his workstation. His moronic boss had insisted that this trivial angle bracket job had to be finished today, *No matter what!*

He threw the papers down on the worktable and donned his welding jacket, helmet and gloves. With growing irritation, Doug aligned the first pieces, clamped them down and attached the grounding electrode. He slipped a fresh welding rod into the handheld electrode.

Doug reached back and flipped the rickety power switch: Nothing.

"Damn it!" He bashed his elbow back against the rusty metal case and the balky machine sputtered and finally started up.

"Piece of crap!"

• • •

"So that's pretty much how it works," Tim O'Keefe beamed as he stroked the rack-mounted computer. "The signal comes in from Modesto to the microwave dish antenna on the old tower next to the shed. Then it's fed into this receiver, processed by the computer and sent to the AM transmitter in this rack. From there it's off to the big tower antenna and out the eager listeners of Northern California."

"Nice," Frank inspected the refrigerator-sized racks of electronics that filled the room. "And the power for everything?" he finally asked.

"Ah; come with me."

The two middle-aged men left the warm confines of the radio control room. They walked the short distance to the low building next door. Tim carefully selected the proper key from his copious collection, squatted down and unclasped the three very sturdy padlocks that secured the bottom of the robust roll-up door. The man heaved mightily and the heavy door rattled upward.

Yet another stout door stood just behind the hefty roll-up.

Tim unlocked the second steel access door, deactivated the alarm system and ventured into the dim chamber.

"What's with the double metal doors on these two buildings?"

Tim frowned. "Unattended transmitters sites always seem to suffer from the same two afflictions: vandals and vermin." He reached for the light switch. "Hunters and metal scavengers are always trying to break in for some reason. This site also has a huge problem with ground squirrels."

28

"Those cute little fluffy guys that we saw on the trip up here?" Frank asked incredulously.

"Yeah; squirrels." Tim shook his head in disgust, "Six months ago, they chewed through some brand new underground power cables and shut down the transmitter for three days. Old Lloyd Gozport was furious. It cost him five thousand dollars in lost revenue and eighteen thousand for the repairs."

Tim rapped his knuckles against the solid cinder block walls, "That's why all of the new stuff up here is built so well. It keeps out vermin and vandals."

Frank studied the austere chamber. "Mmm; it is heavy duty."

Tim chuckled and pointed upward, "Even the roof is bulletproof."

Frank pried open the industrial gray cover of the main electrical panel and examined the columns of circuit breakers, "Where is the backup power?"

"Behind that door," he gestured to the right. "There's a big engine-generator and a battery bank to keep everything running if the power goes out. We've got enough propane in the tank to run the transmitter at half power for 72 hours."

On the Back of the Beast

TJ timidly joined the older men in the dim bunker. Tim turned to his son, "What's up?"

The young man rubbed his forehead, "Can you help me get these things into the shipping crate?"

Tim smiled at Frank; "I'll leave you to your work, Mr. Johnson. I've got to help the kid pack up the last of the parts from the old transmitter." He chuckled, "Lloyd is trying to sell the junk on eBay as antiques."

• • •

Long before it arrived at the construction site, Gary and the two laborers could hear the burly roar of the Jaguar as it rumbled up the hill. The three men watched with interest from the high ground of the roof as the red sports car pulled into the dusty circular driveway. The elegant curved lines of the machine were finally interrupted when the driver's door opened and an exquisite woman emerged.

"¡Mira! Es una chica," Luis said.

The woman appraised the unfinished structure with a smug grin.

"Can I help you?" Gary called down to the interloper.

The woman's dark maned head tilted leisurely upward and a pleasant grin appeared. "Hello;" her dark eyebrows arched up, "I have some drawings for you boys."

Gary unhitched his tool belt, "I'll be right down."

By the time that he had reached the driveway, the visitor had retrieved a thick roll of white paper from the car. He held out his hand in greeting, "I'm Gary Hendley, the lead carpenter."

"Good to meet you," she lightly tapped at his calloused outstretched palm with her manicured fingers. "I'm Cat Torres, the Architect for this posh little shack."

She presented the drawings to him.

Gary unfurled the scroll and studied the first sheet with interest, "I don't see a Planning Department OK on these changes. Has the city approved this yet?"

"Don't worry; they will," the woman chortled. "With my stamp on the drawings, they will approve pretty much anything."

She raised her hand and fluttered her fingers coquettishly, "Bye now. Enjoy the drawings."

The tall woman glided away.

Gary watched Cat drive off as he stood burdened
with the heavy set of plans flapping in the wind.
A loud whistle from above interrupted his
daydream. He turned to gazed up at the two men
who were gawking on the roof.

"¡Qué bonita!" Luis nodded approvingly.

"Back to work you perverts!" Gary shouted. "I
want you guys to clean up the job site for
tomorrow." He winced and added, "But first let's
take a fifteen minute break, I've gotta pee really
bad."

• • •

The First Officer switched them to Bay Area Air
Traffic Control as the huge plane neared the
jagged coast of California, "OK Captain Weaver,
we're good to come straight into SFO on
Runway 1 Right with our low fuel warning."
After the long monotony of the Pacific crossing,
the man yawned. "On the plus side, Burt, we'll
be landing twenty minutes early. You'll be home
with Nancy by noon."

"Thanks Dick." The Captain struggled to shake
off the heavy sense of portents that had hung
over him during most of the flight. He activated
the cabin PA system, "Flight crew, prepare for

landing." His fingers toggled several switches and the jet locked into the landing approach.

Just as the silver craft crossed high over the beach at Pillar Point, the belly of the plane splayed open and the landing gears reached down into the turbulent air.

5. The beast stirs

"That'll be two dollars, Mr. Bradshaw," Ida informed the elderly gentleman who waited at the checkout counter.

The thin old man reached into his pants pocket, produced two bills and handed them to her with a grin, "I'm feeling lucky, Mrs. Martinez."

She took the crumbled banknotes and passed two scratcher lottery tickets to the customer, "Good luck."

The man laid the cards on the counter and rubbed off the dull silver paint that covered most of the surface. His shoulders slumped, "Nothing today." He slipped the useless tickets into his pocket and wandered out of the deserted market.

Ida followed him to the glass door, twisted the 'Open' sign around to 'Closed' and latched the lock. She had so much merchandise to shelve today. The woman dragged two boxes of *Blitz Straight Whiskey* and the small aluminum stepladder from the back room. She set four hip flasks of liquor on the top step of the ladder and carefully ascended the wobbly steps.

Ida brushed the dust from the high display shelf and reached down for the first of the glass bottles.

The stepladder quivered strangely.

The building jerked brutally upward, propelling Ida Martinez and much of the contents of the market towards the ceiling. Deep in the earth below her, the beast that is the Hayward fault lurched free of its uneasy slumber. A massive earthquake was now inescapable.

Ida's head impacted the plaster of the ceiling. She could hear the hideous crack of bones in her skull and neck. In the fraction of a second that it took to fall, she watched dispassionately as the oscillating floor bolted up to meet her.

IMPACT.

For an instant, the brawling violence of the beast subsided.

Ida laid crumbled on the floor in the havoc of the shattered market. She couldn't move. Her legs and torso were oddly entangled above in the wreckage of the metal ladder.

Blood was everywhere. Her blood, she realized.

The sickening convulsions resumed.

Ida Martinez watched unflinchingly as the remaining items on the high shelves plummeted towards her.

On the Back of the Beast

The tattered and gray shopkeeper was killed
three seconds later when the roof of the old
Fruitvale District market collapsed.

• • •

The arc of incandescent metal played across the
angle iron workpiece with a crackly buzz. Doug
flipped up the darkened faceplate and inspected
the still-glowing object. Not his best work, but it
would still pass quality control. He yanked the
hot grounding electrode free from the piece. He
had finished about a third of the work in just
under an hour.

Maybe he *would* get this all done today.

He assembled another set of parts, lowered the
opaque faceplate and tapped the welding rod to
the metal: Nothing.

"Now what?"

Doug set the electrode aside and checked over
the finicky arc welder. The power switch jiggled
loosely. He'd have to replace it. There was a box
of spares somewhere in the basement, Doug
thought for a moment, in that weird storage
space under the stairs. He stripped off his jacket
and gloves then trotted across the cluttered shop.

His boss frowned disapprovingly as he passed
the office.

36

"I'm almost done." Doug smiled disingenuously, "The switch is busted on the welder. I'm gonna put in a new one."

He bustled down the robust old planks that made up the open stairway to the basement and picked his way though the accumulation of infrequently needed supplies that were stored under it. Doug located a box marked 'Lincoln Main Switches' in the dim light. He retrieved a fat and glossy new device from the carton.

The concrete floor of the basement rippled. The lights vanished. Doug pitched roughly against the bottom of a plank stair tread, "What the..."

In the shop above, he could hear someone shriek. The tremor intensified. He balled himself up in the madly flailing maelstrom under the basement stairs. The ancient brick building that housed Harmon Weld Shop disintegrated. Tons of ragged masonry and shredded wood fell into the wide concrete-lined pit of the basement. Dust and smoke nearly smothered him. Something sharp stabbed repeatedly at his left leg.

Again and again he was pummeled in the dark.

• • •

"Alright; who's the line leader today?" Mrs. Cunningham queried the wiggly Second Graders who waited at the door to be dismissed for recess.

Nicholas haltingly raised his hand from the front of the line.

Gwen's slim fingers slid up Fiona's back and tugged lightly on her blonde hair.

Fiona spun around and smirked, "The Monkey Bars, right?"

Gwen nodded.

Mrs. Cunningham frowned, "We're waiting for Gwen and Fiona now."

Gwen glanced apprehensively towards the teacher at the end of the line.

"Who can tell me where are our hands are supposed to be while we wait in line?"

"At our sides?" Jason Chan suggested.

Mrs. Cunningham nodded, "At our sides, Gwen and Fiona. Girls, we've talked about putting our hands in other people's hair," she admonished. "If I have to remind you two again, you will miss the next recess."

The classroom jerked startlingly to the left.

Gwen's eyes grew wide as the walls of Room C-1 squeaked and groaned. The girl turned back towards her teacher. Mrs. Cunningham clutched the vibrating wall, her face ashen with terror.

The room shook in horrible heaving waves.

"RUN!" Mrs. Cunningham barked.

Jason Chan and Nicholas managed to pull the door open and the students tumbled out of the now-crumbling wing. Gwen glimpsed the chalkboard separate from the wall and fall heavily across Fiona's desk. Both desk and board split in two. Mrs. Cunningham pushed her hard and she dashed towards the safety of the play structure.

Gwen tripped over Isabelle and plunged to the wildly bouncing tan bark. She squirmed under the huge red slide and wrapped her arms around a wooden support post.

A sharp chunk of serrated metal skittered past her. Bark flew everywhere.

She was dizzy.

Gwen was sure that she would barf as she was slammed against the red slide.

The sounds were terrible: screaming kids, crashing buildings, breaking glass.

On the Back of the Beast

• • •

At the Port of Oakland, the *Kobe Meteor* snapped its moorings as it careened wildly in the huge seismically induced waves that sloshed swiftly across the wide estuary. The monstrous cargo ship pitched and yawed ponderously, flinging steel boxes and men into the surrounding watery tumult. The vessel bashed repeatedly against the unforgiving concrete dock before it rolled sideways and crushed Victor Mills and sixteen other unlucky Longshoremen.

A mile and a quarter inland, Lisa Mills was summarily slammed against the huge plate glass window in the office break room by a heavy wooden lunch table. Lisa screamed for an instant before the shear strength of the tempered pane was significantly exceeded by the crushing weight of the woman and table. Trapped against the window, Lisa Mills was propelled into the gushy morning air twelve stories above the business district of Oakland.

The bizarre sandwich of glass, human and furniture hurdled across the street far below before it shattered against an overturned delivery truck.

Unwittingly, Gwen Mills was now one of thousands of new orphans.

• • •

Kayla Hendley opened her tear-swollen eyes as she lay somberly on the sofa in the Counseling Office. Far in the distance she could hear a deep growling rumble. When the glass partitions clattered, Kayla sat up, expecting the return of the long-delayed Counselor. Though the quivering window she could see the school secretary staggering around her gyrating desk. Filing cabinets and bookshelves collided. Heavy ancient light fixtures crashed down.

The office darkened. Kayla gripped the side of the bucking sofa. The windows shrieked painfully before they exploded into a barrage of flying fragments. The ceiling ripped open above her and briefly spilled light onto the panicky secretary who wobbled around in the ruins of the school office.

A thick roof beam dropped and finally dispatched the star-crossed office worker.

A heavy section of the now-unsupported roof collapsed and flattened the remainder of the badly damaged school office.

• • •

Gary Hendley sat on the filthy gray toilet seat of the fetid job site PortiJohn. He sighed with relief as he finished up his business.

The little plastic building jerked sideways.

41

On the Back of the Beast

Gary fleetingly clutched the commode seat in fear.

"Hey;" he shouted, "knock it off, Luis!"

Curiously, in the distance he could hear the man franticly yelling in Spanish. Something had apparently gone wrong; probably one of the stupid practical jokes. Gary stood and fastened his pants. Someone might well lose their job today if things were really screwed up. He slid the latch and kicked open the door.

Gary was wrenched savagely to the side. "EARTHQUAKE!" he shouted to the laborers. He tumbled flimsily about in the dirt and construction debris. Gary saw the north wing of the unfinished building shear off and crash down in a jumble of splintered wood. An explosion nearby reverberated around the steep slopes of the Oakland Hills.

The ground split into wide rifts and spastically disembarked down the precarious terrain as rock slides. Even through the thunderous pandemonium, Gary could hear a car alarm whining in the distance.

Most of the rest of the mansion that he had worked on for months wracked incessantly from side to side before it twisted unnaturally around and disintegrated.

S F Chapman

This is a bad one, Gary thought as his head was walloped by the shuddering earth.

• • •

Cat Torres stomped on the gas pedal and the Jaguar rocketed up the on-ramp to Highway 24.

The broad ascending curve of the freeway led to the four bores of the Caldacott tunnel as it pierced the Oakland Hills between Berkeley and Orinda. The mid-morning traffic was routinely constricted to twin lanes to allow for maintenance work and today was no exception.

She playfully dodged between lanes in the nimble red roadster to avoid pockets of congestion.

Ahead, a double trailer laden semi lumbered into the murky tunnel. Cat accelerated to meet the challenge of overtaking the mammoth vehicle. The sports car shot forward. With a triumphant grin, Cat was nearly past the cab of the truck. The Jag bucked and shimmied, nearly veering into the tall left-hand curb.

"Damned exhaust valves!" She released the gas pedal and the bucking stopped.

The truck wobbled oddly and drifted inexorably into the lane in front of her. Cat pounded the car horn and stomped the brakes but a headlong

43

crash with the side of the long trailer was inevitable.

The semi skidded sideways and jammed the narrow passage. Inexplicably the car was flung airborne, its sleek red hood sailed toward the broadside of the first trailer.

Cat clenched the steering wheel in horror.

The lights in the tunnel flickered off. With a shriek of grinding metal, the red XKE barreled into the swaying truck.

Cat's forehead smashed the wooden grip of the steering wheel.

Shards of glass shot past her in the smoky darkness.

The remains of the slaughtered Jaguar tumbled several times before it came to rest. Steam sizzled from the torn radiator. Gyrating waves of buckling pavement swarmed through the clogged passageway.

As she was bludgeoned around in the wrecked roadster, Cat could hear other vehicles colliding in the calamitously undulating tunnel.

• • •

Captain Weaver watched the little commuter plane in the distance cross over the left side runway markings of the long parallel landing strips. The small aircraft would likely be well out of the way when the behemoth jumbo jet descended upon the opposite runway. The pilot adjusted the trim of the sluggish plane to compensate for gusty northerly winds as he gauged the centerline markings of Runway 1 Right.

Captain Weaver slowly reduced the airspeed and rotated the nose of the 747 up. They were aligned for a perfect landing. Just below, the shops and eating establishments of downtown Millbrae raced by. The jet howled across Highway 101 at one hundred and seventy-five miles per hour and hurtled over the orderly yellow chevrons of the airport Blast Pads.

"LOOK!" the First Officer screamed.

A mile and a half down the slender ribbons of concrete, the commuter plane cartwheeled sideways along the taxiway.

Gravity and declining airspeed continued to tug the gargantuan airliner towards the writhing runway.

The pilot yanked the throttles to FULL and the four giant GEnx engines lazily revved up.

On the Back of the Beast

"OH, CRAP!"

Captain Weaver jerked the Control Yoke for an emergency landing abort. "We're gonna hit the runway before we get back up!"

The descending aircraft shuddered and roared with the titanic battle between gravity and engine thrust.

"Slats and flaps!" the Captain shouted.

The left wing dropped suddenly towards the ground. Debris pelted the undercarriage. The rear left wheels struck the upsurging pavement and the craft stumbled alarmingly.

A fist-sized fragment of rubble collided with the franticly spinning fan blades of the Number Two engine. The finely crafted turbine shattered in a chaotic torrent of hot and frenzied metal.

"Go, Go, GO!" the pilot implored.

The maimed metal albatross floundered skyward.

The Captain wrestled for control of the badly damaged plane. The two men panted with exhaustion. At least for now, all 493 on board the slowly ascending aircraft had been spared.

"Burt!" the First Officer pointed to the twin runways.

S F Chapman

The bay waters roiled furiously, driving wave after wave across the lowlands that contained San Francisco International Airport.

As they rose back to the safety of the air, Captain Weaver watched the overturned commuter plane rotate slowly in an eddy before it broke up under a mountain of angry gray water.

6. 10:21 AM: Escape!

The Passenger Cabin Message Light blinked relentlessly.

"Engine Two is down. The landing gears won't retract. There's no ground radar beacons," the First Officer inventoried the condition of the hobbled craft. "I can't pick up Air Traffic Control."

Captain Weaver strained to keep the plane airborne, "Dick; we've got to get this heap on the ground!"

The jumbo jet teetered over the bay's frothy gray uproar of breakers.

The First Officer checked the conditions on the ground, "Oakland International is a mess."

"What about San Jose?"

"I see flames;" he stared out of the window to the south, "and a huge cloud of black smoke. I think some of the fuel storage tanks have exploded."

"Where the hell are we going to land?" the pilot huffed in frustration.

"Reno or Sacramento?"

"Reno's out. We've still got a big fuel problem and I doubt we could coax this wreck over the Sierras." The pilot glanced at the rim of ridges that loomed ahead, "It may not make it over the Berkeley Hills."

• • •

The shaking finally stopped in the dark tunnel.

That wasn't just the Jag and the truck that collided, Cat realized. It must have been an earthquake!

She brushed several fingers over her throbbing brow. A slick mixture of blood and grit dribbled down her face.

She was wedged sideways against the driver's door of the ruined Jaguar in the smoky blackness of the ravaged tunnel. Cat could hear a woman scream in the distance.

A tiny aftershock set the car trembling again.

She had to get out!

Cat felt around in the oppressive gloom. The Alternator light flickered weakly on the console and revealed hazards everywhere. She slipped free of the seatbelt, twisted around and gingerly crawled back towards the rear hatch. She slowly probed around the edge of the distorted rear window frame for unseen hazards. Cat carefully pulled herself free of the smashed car.

She winced as she stood up in the littered tunnel. Something had pierced her left foot. Cat slid her hand downward. One shoe was missing. She grimaced as she plucked a long jagged shard of something from her bare foot.

Cat feared that she would soon be entombed in the dark underground passage. She squirmed past the decimated truck. A short distance ahead in the nightmarish haze she could see the tunnel opening.

She made her way past fallen rubble and several crushed vehicles. In the dim light, she stopped to investigate an overturned car. Pressed behind the deflated air bag were the mangled remains of the dead driver. She winced and hobbled past the morbid scene. A half dozen traumatized and confused people loitered around the entrance to the tunnel.

Cat stared in shock at the heavy destruction that surrounded the tunnel entrance. The long graceful curve of the freeway approach was now a jumble of smashed vehicles and upended concrete. It must have been a huge earthquake, she realized. Emergency assistance would be unlikely for days, if not weeks.

The band of stunned tunnel survivors murmured and speculated about the disaster. An ashen old man stopped Cat and dabbled at her forehead with a grimy beach towel. She smiled with thanks but the impassive man staggered away to tend to another victim.

The rumbling began anew and the little group around the portal quickly dispersed. Cat limped off between the dozens of askew cars and traumatized motorists that were scattered around the fractured freeway.

A few hundred feet away an overturned and burning minivan sputtered and crackled while a bruised young woman clutched two dazed children nearby.

A teenage boy trotted up and pulled the dumbstruck group away from the intensifying inferno. Cat vacillated about whether or not to assist the dozens of victims. There seemed to be no shortage of the able-bodied. She'd probably be more of a hindrance than help. Cat plodded away. If she could find some shoes, she'd hike over the hills and return home.

• • •

Doug wheezed in the dark and dusty air. He pushed aside several cardboard boxes and retrieved the cell phone from his pants pocket. Eerie bluish light from the device spilled about in the claustrophobic cave. Fine particles of floating detritus glinted in the air.

Searching for signal scrolled across the phone's screen. Doug held the device up and shone the dim light around his tiny prison. There was rubble everywhere. He rechecked the screen: *Signal not found* blinked ominously. In the diminishing light, he pawed at the wall of broken masonry that blocked his exit. There didn't seem to be any way out.

He forced the fallen supplies sideways and sat up. Doug could hear running water and odd groaning noises. He smelled something. Was it Natural gas? Just before the cell phone's battery failed and with it the tenuous light, he noticed a rivulet of brown water had seeped in.

As Doug sat trapped in the black crypt under the remains of Harmon Weld Shop, water had already pooled up around him.

• • •

Captain Weaver fought with the flight controls of the damaged airliner.

The First Officer activated the PA system. "Ladies and gentleman; we are diverting to Sacramento because of a runway emergency at San Francisco International. The Captain has ordered that all passengers and crew must remain seated with seatbelts fastened until further notice."

• • •

"TJ!" Tim shouted at the heap of fractured wood that was the remains of the old transmitter shack.

"Yeah Dad?" a muffled voice answered from the pile.

"We're gonna try to lift this section of the roof," Tim cupped his ear and waited.

"OK; I think I can help."

Frank Johnson and Tim O'Keefe hoisted the hulking remnant and the young man thrashed free.

TJ brushed his hair back and squinted at the demolished structure, "When the shaking started, I ducked next to the shipping crate and held on." He shook his head in amazement, "It probably saved my life."

"You were lucky," Frank nodded, "I got knocked on my ass in the Generator Room. I kept slamming into something in the dark."

They turned to Tim for his survivor's tale.

"Don't look at me. I just bounced around like a tennis ball on the asphalt."

Tim picked a long splinter out of his left palm, "Everyone's been expecting a big earthquake for years, but you just never think it's really going to happen." Tim withdrew the slender dagger of wood and flicked it away, "That was one helluva quake, the biggest I've ever felt."

The man frowned, "Where is the Jeep?"

The three men scanned the transmitter site. A large slab of pavement had sheared off and disappeared where the SUV had been parked.

"TJ;" Tim directed, "go over and take a look."

"OK Dad." The young man ambled away.

Tim smirked, "Was that your first earthquake, Mr. Johnson?"

"Yeah;" Frank confessed, "it was quite a doozy."

TJ hiked back to the older men, "Everything slid down about two hundred feet. The Cherokee is stuck under a big hunk of blacktop and some busted trees."

"Well;" Tim winced, "we ain't gettin' out of here by Jeep, I guess."

"Dad;" TJ interjected, "did you guys look around? The whole Bay Area is destroyed. There's a brunch of fires and smoke..."

A faint mechanical buzz was followed by the muffled sound of an engine starting. The men stared at each other in alarm. The commotion had come from the wrong direction to be the stranded vehicle.

"What the hell is that?" Frank asked.

A siren warbled in the wind. Tim's forehead wrinkled and he turned towards the low gray buildings. "The backup generator's firing up."

He tilted his head and thought for a moment, "When the power goes out, the transmitter shuts down and the electronics switch to batteries. After five minutes, the backup generator kicks in and the transmitter resets." The man grinned with surprise, "Son of a bitch! It should be broadcasting again!"

The excitement was short lived. Frank pointed to the remains of the old antenna by the collapsed shack. The microwave dish that received the signal from Modesto had toppled over.

Tim and TJ stared at Frank.

"Now what?"

7. Imminent conflagrations

She'd carried the right shoe for at least a half an hour, Cat realized. Its twin was lost somewhere in the Caldacott tunnel during the earthquake.

After a quarter of a mile of stumbling up a road that would eventually take her over the steep hills, she'd pulled off the remaining shoe.

Cat stopped and slumped against a buckled metal guardrail. This was going to be much more difficult than she had expected.

A trail of bloody footprints stretched out behind her.

She bent down and brushed bits of crimson gravel from her abraded soles.

Cat contemplated the forlorn footwear in her hand. The single shoe was only half of a two hundred dollar set. Why was she still lugging it along?

With a scornful cackle, she flung the beige leather low top down the precipitous hillside.

She watched for several seconds as the shoe tumbled downward.

There would have to be another way to reach her goal.

She had already backtracked around a landslide, worked her way across a hundred foot section of shredded pavement and clambered over a toppled retaining wall. The tedious nine mile trudge back to her home in Lafayette would likely take days.

Blood still dribbled from her left heel.

Cat had seen no one since she left the zombie-like group at the tunnel.

Well; no one alive, she corrected herself. The legs of some unfortunate soul had protruded from the bottom of the fallen retaining wall.

She needed some sort of wrap for her lame foot.

She picked at the waist of her blue blouse. "100% cotton, only the best quality," Cat remembered the saleswoman had told her.

Cat fiddled with it for several minutes and was eventually able to tear a long wide strip of the thin material from the bottom edge of the garment.

She tied the improvised bandage securely around her injured foot and wobbled away.

After several minutes of slow and downtrodden progress, she heard the horn blare from an approaching vehicle. A worn out old pickup crept towards her.

The rumbly truck stopped.

"Ms Torres?" a man called from the cab.

Cat studied the battered truck and the beleaguered driver. It was Jerry or Gary, the carpenter from the mansion, she couldn't quite remember his name.

Maybe her dismal situation had improved.

She forced a friendly smile, "Hi; how are you doing?"

A particularly distressed man sat up in the bed of the pickup, "¡Vamos! We gotta go!" he implored the driver.

"Yeah; I know Luis," the driver nodded gravely. "Do you need any help Ms Torres?"

"I think so," she sheepishly admitted. "I'm trying to walk over the hills to Lafayette. But I lost my shoes in the earthquake."

Cat glanced down at the ruby streaked wrapping that covered her left foot. "It's not going really well."

58

"I've got an old pair of rain boots, do you want them?" The man grimaced, "Do you need something for that gash on your forehead too?"

After dealing with the travails of her lacerated feet, Cat had forgotten about the throbbing pain in her temple. Her shoulders sagged in defeat, "Can you help me?"

"Sure. Get in."

She struggled around the back of the truck. The man in the bed looked up momentarily as he lingered over a ghastly looking outstretched young man. Cat climbed into the cab. A roll of paper towels and dirt stained black rain boots sat in the center of the bench seat.

The driver resumed the careful journey down the hill, "We've gotta take Alex to the hospital." He shook his head, "But I don't think he'll make it. After that, I'm heading out to Walnut Creek to get my daughter at school."

The pickup jolted over a wide split in the pavement.

"What happened to the boy in the back?" Cat asked.

"His brother says that he was on the roof when the shaking started," the driver inched over a second wide rift in the road, "somehow he ended up under a bunch of debris on the ground."

She studied the man as he concentrated on the arduous task of driving. "Maybe it was the blow to the head, but I can't remember your name," Cat finally admitted.

"Gary Hendley." He shifted warily into second gear, "Your name's Cat, right? Where were you when it hit?"

"Ooohh;" she groaned, "I crashed that fabulous red Jag of mine into a tractor-trailer in the Caldacott."

Cat stared forlornly out the windshield, "I'm going to miss that car." She pressed a square of paper towel against her brow. "What about you, Gary?"

The man laughed unexpectedly, "I've got the worst earthquake survivor story ever." A chagrined look crossed his face; "I was sitting on the can when it hit. If I hadn't jumped out of the PortiJohn, I'd be covered in crap!"

Cat cringed as she scrubbed the dried blood with the paper towel, "What about the other guy in the back of the truck?"

"Luis was the only really lucky one. He was climbing down a ladder from the roof and jumped the last few feet. He's just got a few scratches."

Cat lowered the passenger side sun visor and studied the jagged gash in the vanity mirror, "Under better conditions, I'd get this stitched up. Preferably by a good Plastic Surgeon." She continued to probe lightly with the towel, "What happened to the mansion?"

"Totaled."

"I was afraid of that," she thought for a moment, "I don't think my business liability insurance covers earthquake damage."

"It's not going to matter," he pressed on the brakes and the pickup stopped, "when we left the site, there was a big fire down the street and another one up on the ridge."

The road ahead was split into a wide chasm filled with huge broken puzzle pieces of blacktop.

"With the wind today," Gary noted, "nothing will survive the firestorm that's gonna develop."

"Firestorm?"

"Remember the Hiller Heights Fire in 1991? That was in this part of the hills and it destroyed everything."

"*That's right,*" Cat shuddered with the sudden stark realization, "I would have walked right into it."

On the Back of the Beast

· · ·

"I think that it'll work," Frank Johnson said doubtfully as he stared at the tangle of improvised parts tenuously connected to the rack-mounted computer.

Sixty-seven minutes earlier, he and Tim O'Keefe had convinced each other that they could rig up a makeshift radio studio and broadcast emergency messages using the idle transmitter. Tim and TJ had pried apart a cell phone in search of a microphone, but the effort had not yielded anything usable. TJ eventually found the handset from an ancient rotary dial desk phone in the ruins of the old transmitter shed.

Tim had carefully shaved off the plastic insulation from the last several inches of the coiled beige cord. Frank used white adhesive tape to attach the wires to the audio input connectors on the computer's motherboard.

Tim fiddled with the computer monitor, "Alright; we will ignore the missing Microwave signal." He scrolled the mouse down the screen, "Open the computer audio menu." He looked over to the engineer, "Should we use the microphone setting or audio line-in with this thing?"

Frank shrugged, "With a carbon mike from a

telephone, I'm guessing the microphone setting would work best." He scratched the back of his head, "Without a preamp, we'll probably have to turn the volume up to full."

A small aftershock tousled the cinder block building. Tim reached up and steadied the vibrating monitor, "How are we gonna know if it works?"

TJ smiled, "I'll go listen on the Jeep's radio."

"Good idea, son."

While Frank waited at the double steel doors, Tim followed his son to the broken edge of the asphalt and TJ hiked down to the smashed vehicle. After several minutes, Tim waved to Frank and the engineer switched on the jury-rigged broadcasting system.

He lifted the heavy handset and watched through the door for Tim's reaction, "Testing. Testing. Can you hear me TJ?"

Tim spun around and grinned. He pointed his thumbs up in victory.

With a sudden wave of stage fright, Frank was starkly aware that he could now be heard by perhaps thousands of unseen listeners. "Uh...This is Frank Johnson...I'm at the mountaintop transmitter for AM radio 600...ah..."

On the Back of the Beast

Tim O'Keefe chuckled as he returned to the building. "I was a radioman on the Midway during the Vietnam War," he whispered to the faltering amateur announcer, "do you want me to take over?"

Frank passed the handset to him.

"Hello; this is Tim O'Keefe. We are now broadcasting emergency information at six hundred kilohertz Amplitude Modulation from 27 miles northeast of San Francisco, California." He checked the output meter, "We are currently at 5,200 watts of effective power. Shortly, we will report on the various conditions that we can see from the mountaintop following the massive earthquake that shook the area at about 10:17 AM Pacific Daylight time."

In only few minutes the three men developed a good system to broadcast news of the disaster. TJ would use the binoculars that he found in the Jeep to study a problem area far below. Tim would make general observations about the weather conditions and the many aftershocks from the open doorway. TJ would trot in, hand the binoculars to Frank and describe what he had just witnessed. Frank would start a new observation of a different trouble spot.

"The main worry right now seems to be fires," TJ told the radio audience. "I've been watching several smoky fires in the Oakland hills. A couple of them have recently merged together. If you're in the hills, GET OUT. I can't stress this enough, with all of the wind today, it's gonna get really bad..."

A huge boom reverberated across the mountaintop.

Tim rushed to the door, while TJ held the handset in panic.

A massive cloud of roiling black smoke rose in the northwest before being buffeted and distorted by the gusty winds.

Frank hurried back to the building with a look of horror on his face. TJ gave the microphone to the man, "That big oil refinery near the bridge just exploded." He pressed his eyes closed and composed himself, "I've been watching several small fires in that area off and on for awhile. But something has apparently just gone terribly wrong. It's a huge conflagration now." Frank stood in stunned silence, the handset still pressed to his head.

Tim stared at the shaken man and reached out to retrieve the microphone, "We will continue to report on the developing problems with the various fires shortly." He turned to his son, "Do you have anything new, TJ?"

"Yeah; a half an hour ago, a huge passenger plane flew quite low through the valley below us. It seemed really messed up. There was a long stream of smoke trailing out of one engine. I watched it for a few minutes as it headed out towards the Central Valley."

"Thanks TJ. The winds are now blowing some of the refinery smoke our way..."

8. Grueling struggles

The wounded jetliner grazed over a low spot in the Berkeley Hills and sheared off the fluttering tips of several tall pines. Smoke rose everywhere from the countless fires below.

"Ah!" the First Officer exclaimed in victory, "I've got a couple of mobile radar beacons. Apparently there's some helicopters in the air to the north."

Captain Weaver studied the terrain. The saw-toothed hills that surround the bay dropped off on the eastern side into precipitous canyons before they softened in the distance to well-rounded foothills near the river delta. The earthen dam that restrained the Briones reservoir had failed and a turbulent ribbon of muddy water plunged down the steep incline.

With the heavy winds and the damaged engine, the cumbersome craft was buffeted unpredictably. At least we have some altitude to allow for corrections now, the pilot thought.

Below he could see that many vehicles were crushed under several bridges that had fallen onto Highway 24, blocking the heavily traveled thoroughfare to San Francisco. He'd have to find a different route to work.

On the Back of the Beast

A half-dozen fire trucks with flashing red lights blocked the main street through the town of Lafayette. The men below directed several puny streams of water at a block-long inferno.

The usually uniform rails of the BART tracks squiggled and swerved. A long commuter train lay overturned across the disrupted right of way.

Wide areas of Walnut Creek and Pleasant Hill were in ruins. Eruptions of thick black smoke roiled up from the devastation.

The staunch twin peaks of Mt. Diablo towered ahead. They would soon struggle past the north side towards Sacramento, but Burt Weaver's home was in Alamo on the south slope.

"Dick;" the Captain called to the busy First Officer, "look out your window and tell me what it looks like in my neighborhood."

The man twisted his head from side to side, "I see smoke and flames. It doesn't look promising."

The First Officer returned to his fuel calculations.

The pilot suspected that flames would eventually consume his home. Hopefully, he thought, Nancy had escaped unharmed. He banked to the left and headed towards the gap in the foothills that would eventually take them to the wide Central Valley.

"I've got good news and bad news," the First Officer announced.

"Good news first, please."

"I picked up Emergency Air Traffic Control in Sacramento. There's priority landing for flights diverted from the Bay Area."

"Finally something is going our way," Captain Weaver mumbled. "And the bad news?"

"We won't have enough fuel to make it there."

• • •

The unkempt man glanced warily around the nearly deserted downtown Oakland street from the rear of the overturned truck. He suspected that the cops would soon start shooting at looters and he wanted to be done with his dirty deeds by then. The delivery truck had proved to be a disappointing jumble of boxes. The four packages that he had slit open contained nothing of value.

The driver was nowhere to be found in the wreck. The scavenger climbed out of the back of the truck. Glass and shattered furniture littered the street around the vehicle.

Oh, what's this? he thought.

The shredded corpse of a middle age woman lay crumpled under a wide fractured tabletop. He hoisted the damaged table and pushed it to the side. The man looked cautiously up and down the street again before defiling the dead body. He set to work rifling through her tattered clothing.

Easy pickings....

Afterwards he strolled away with a merry little smirk. He'd gotten a cell phone, ten dollars and eighty-one cents in change, and a driver's license for someone named Lisa Mills off of the carcass.

Trembling began anew. He crouched down and rode out the heavy aftershock. This was all good for the thieving business, he thought.

Bring it on Baby!

• • •

Doug couldn't stop shivering in the waist-high putrid water that had steadily risen in the darkened space under the basement stairs. This was not his idea of a good day at work: a butthead boss, brutal shaking, then slow freezing followed by probable drowning.

How long had it been? He had no way of knowing. He tried to count his heartbeats but kept losing track. Had it been ten minutes or two hours?

The water was most likely from a broken pipe, a sewer pipe by the smell of it. The flatlands of Berkeley were at the bottom of hundreds of miles of sewer lines, he mused. It would take days for all of the effluent to drain out. And it seemed to all be gushing into the basement under the recently defunct Harmon Welding.

Doug had slipped under the numbing water during the last aftershock. When he finally got himself upright, coughing and gasping the whole time, his eyes were searing with agony. He'd probably go blind, *if* he survived.

His teeth chattered uncontrollably now. Doug's shoulders and chest had cramped. His hands seemed puffy and useless, like frigid fat mittens at the ends of his fatigued arms.

Doug took a deep breath and tried to relax. He might still get lucky and somehow be rescued.

Hopefully Gary and Kayla were fairing better.

• • •

"A little farther," Cat yelled to Gary from in front of the truck. "STOP! Now turn as far as you can to the left."

On the Back of the Beast

Gary nodded from the cab. They had struggled their way across the narrow broken shoulder of the collapsed roadway.

Luis craned his head from the bed of the barely moving truck and called to the driver, "¡Aye Dios mio! How much longer?"

"We're working on it, Luis," Gary called back. "I wanna get out of here too and find my daughter."

Cat squatted down and looked under the truck, "SLOW GARY! *Really* slow." She stood and motioned him forward.

Gary stifled a laugh when her head popped up; with the dirty rain boots, torn blue blouse and large scabby brown head wound, she was barely recognizable as the elegant and well-coiffed architect from earlier in the day.

"Right a little bit. GOOD! Now straight."

She trotted back to the cab. "I think we did it, just stay to the side for about twenty feet." Cat twisted up her nose, "I can *really* smell the smoke now."

"Hopefully that will be the last of our difficulties."

9. The improvised rescue squad

The aftershock subsided and the crouching teacher let loose the eight-year-old girl that he'd shielded.

"That wasn't so bad." Mr. Newman checked on the two other helpers, "Are you guys alright?"

Evan and Michael, both gloomy high schoolers, nodded.

"Let's get back to work," The teacher warily eyed the ruins of the Jefferson High School office. "The receptionist said that there should be two people in here somewhere."

Gwen peeked under an immense section of the fallen roof, "I think this is the perfect spot to hunt for someone who's missing."

"I guess it's as good as any," the man assessed the stability of the flattened building. "OK Gwen, be careful," Mr. Newman tapped on the oversized pink bicycle helmet as it drooped slowly down over her eyes.

The boys glanced doubtfully at each other while the little girl adjusted the clumsy headgear.

She switched on the heavy metal flashlight,

scrunched down and peered under the section.
Gwen turned back to the waiting threesome with
an indefatigable grin, "I'm going in boys!"

"Remember what I said," Mr. Newman called
after her as she wriggled into the dark cave of
debris, "if the shaking starts again, drop
everything and hold onto the helmet. I'll try to
pull you out by your feet."

Gwen crawled past the opening and slowly
waved the flashlight from side to side.

"Why is she here with us, Mr. Newman?" Evan
whispered to the teacher.

"We don't have much choice. We need all of the
help we can get and she's very good at these
sorts of things," the man answered. "She and her
dad did some cave exploring during the summer
in New Mexico. She told me that they even
camped out underground for a few days."

Gwen grinned at the teacher's comments as she
shimmied through a tight gap

"Unfortunately," the teacher added, "time is
running out for any trapped survivors."

Gwen swept aside some broken glass, pried back
a splintered board and slithered up into a wide
gray chamber.

"How's it going in there?" Mr. Newman call to her.

"Pretty good. I'm still looking." She swiveled the light around in the cavern. Gwen frowned, *what was that spooky sound?* The troublesome helmet slowly sank and eclipsed her view.

There it was again.

"Mr. Newman, I hear something!"

"What?"

"Ahh;" she shouted, "it sounds like moaning!"

"Are you sure?"

She tilted her head sideways to locate the source of the weird undertone. Gwen lifted the brim of the pink helmet and shone the flashlight deep into the rubble-strewn space.

Something moved.

"I FOUND SOMEONE!" she yelled.

"Can you get to the person?" Mr. Newman called out.

Gwen zigzagged past a big beam and snaked forward to a heap of fallen ceiling tiles, "Yeah; just barely."

On the Back of the Beast

She picked through a mound of shredded white pressboard. Gwen carefully spread apart tangled and dusty ribbons of matted brown hair to reveal the dusty face of an unconscious young woman.

Gwen shone the flashlight at the stricken teen. The victim's eyes flickered open unexpectedly. Both rescuer and victim shrieked with surprise.

"GWEN!" Mr. Newman shouted, "What's going on?"

The teenager flinched in pain, "Am I...dead?"

The little girl studied the bigger one in earnest for a moment, "No; I think you're OK."

"GWEN!" the teacher bellowed.

"We've got to get this person out of here, Mr. Newman." Gwen gently wiped sand away from the eyes of the immobile survivor. "Can you talk?"

The teen coughed and wheezed which caused a mini blizzard of swirling dust, "Uh...barely."

"What's your name?" the little girl asked.

"Ka...Kayla."

"My name is Gwen," she said with satisfaction.

"Did you get hurt in the earthquake?"

"Earthquake?" Kayla asked in confusion. "My...arm. My left arm is killing me."

Through the snarl of fallen rubble they could hear the teacher, "Michael, Evan! There's a survivor over here!"

Gwen pulled herself directly above the teenager's entrapped head. The large pink helmet drifted downward to conceal the little rescuer's eyes.

Kayla was momentarily charmed by her plucky savior.

"We'll get you out of this mess," Gwen resolutely told the young woman.

After twenty minutes of careful excavation work, the improvised rescue squad discovered that a stout beam had fallen on Kayla's arm. Her left hand was hideously crimson and swollen.

Mr. Newman studied the crushed appendage, "Can you wiggle your fingers?"

Kayla grimaced, "No."

"I don't like the look of that;" the teacher muttered, "hopefully the arm can be saved."

On the Back of the Beast

Gwen hovered protectively over the stricken teenager while Evan and Mr. Newman wrestled the beam off of the girl's arm. She was finally free.

Tiny cascades of loose detritus slid from Kayla when Gwen helped her to sit up. The teenager screeched in pain and cradled her damaged arm.

With great care, they got the injured teen to her feet.

Michael rejoined the rescuers crowded around Kayla. Gwen noticed the uneasy boy tug at Mr. Newman's arm, "I found the second person. It's the school secretary."

The teacher's eyebrows arched up.

Michael shook his head dolefully. "*Dead,*" he whispered.

Mr. Newman glanced apprehensively down at Gwen. "It's nearly lunch time and I'm sure you're hungry after all of your awesome rescue work." A feigned smile stretched across his face, "Gwen can you help Kayla to the Triage Area across the street at Lincoln Grade School?" He patted her on the back, "You can get something to eat while you're there, sweet pea."

Gwen nodded knowingly, "OK, Mr. Newman."

She led the dazed young woman away.

"Good luck with the dead secretary," the little girl called back to them.

10. News from on high

"I don't know what we're going to do about the fuel problem," Captain Weaver snarled. He eased his strained grip on the controls and considered various options. "Dick; what was the air speed that you used for the calculations?" he finally asked the First Officer.

"Standard cruising speed of 575 knots."

"Mmm; I thought so." The Captain tapped tersely on the center console, "We're barely making 300 knots. And altitude?"

"Well;" the First Officer hedged, "we've been all over the place altitude wise, so I just figured it at a thousand feet."

The pilot slowly nodded, "I think we can *just* make it."

The younger man tipped his head, "How?"

"Other than the landing gears hanging down, we're configured for maximum lift to compensate for the missing engine."

"Right."

"Let's pull in the slats and trim the flaps."

The First Officer shook his head, "We'll just stall and crash."

"No;" the Captain continued, "if we take it right to the edge of stalling, our drag will go way down and we can reduce engine thrust. We'll be able to squeeze a few more miles out of this heap."

"This sounds like an old Navy trick to me," the man mused skeptically. "What the hell! We've got so much going against us now anyhow. It might work."

"Thanks for the overwhelming approval," Captain Weaver snickered. "One more thing, I want you go back into the cabin and check on the condition of the Number Two engine though the passenger windows."

"OK," The First Officer flinched at the request. "I'm sure it's sheer pandemonium in the passenger cabin right now."

"Sorry about that, tell them that everything is under control. See if you can check the rear landing gears too. If you crane your neck, you can see the outside set through a few of the rear windows. I'd like to know if they are damaged or not."

• • •

"...once again, this is AM 600 broadcasting emergency information about the earthquake that occurred this morning." Tim handed the handset to TJ.

"I've seen a lot of helicopters in the air in the last few minutes," the young man reported. "There were two hovering near the hospital. They took turns landing but they didn't stay long."

Tim frowned at the mention of helicopters.

TJ continued, "I have no way of knowing whether they were dropping off victims or evacuating patients." He handed the makeshift microphone back to his father.

"Helicopters," Tim repeated. "If anyone could spare a ride, the three of us are stranded up here on the mountain top. Eventually, I'd like find out what kind of mess awaits me at home."

Frank returned to the doorway and handed the binoculars to TJ.

"We have a new report coming in," Tim announced. "Here's Mr. Johnson."

"Thanks. The refinery fire seems to be spreading into the city of Martinez. Fleeing to the south seems to be the only good option. DO NOT GO WEST. The waterfront area looks really bad."

While Frank continued to report on escape routes, Tim glanced out the door towards the distant firestorm.

"Hopefully the roads are still passable," Frank passed the handset to Tim.

"The winds are really picking up now. We have two major wild fires raging. One at the oil refinery near Martinez and the other sweeping through the Oakland/Berkeley Hills. But we're seeing many smaller fires everywhere," the strain of narrating the far off disaster was affecting Tim. "If firefighters in the outlying areas can hear us, we really need some help.

• • •

The First Officer slammed the cabin door shut and twisted the lock, "Oh, man! The passengers are really agitated." He returned to his seat, "Many of them saw the drama at SFO." He slipped on the headset, "Everyone on the left side has an excellent view of the decimated Number Two engine."

He laughed scornfully, "One guy even demanded that we turn around immediately and fly him back to San Francisco."

"What did it look like out the window?"

On the Back of the Beast

"I don't know how we avoided ditching in the bay," he shook his head. "The engine cowling and exhaust fairing are gone. Most of the intake is shredded and it's still trailing oil and black smoke."

"What about the landing gears?"

"I could barely see them. The cover on the outside left set is damaged but the gear looks OK."

"I talked to the tower at Sacramento." The Captain stared pensively out of the cockpit windows, "They've cleared the runway for a potential crash landing."

"Even more great news," the First Officer scowled.

• • •

Gwen led a still very bewildered Kayla slowly across the side street between Jefferson High School and Lincoln Grade School. A hectic mishmash of mini vans, SUVs and frantic parents filled the Elementary school parking lot in the distance. The girls finally reached the open gate in the sturdy chain link fence that surrounded most of the Grade School.

The burly head janitor stopped them, "What's up ladies?"

"Hi. I'm Gwen Mills. I was helping Mr. Newman search through the high school for survivors."

"How did it go over there?" the big man eyed the disheveled teenager.

"We found one!" Gwen replied with a pleased grin. "Mr. Newman told me to take her to the tree-pause area, but I don't know exactly where that is."

"You mean the Triage Area?"

Gwen nodded.

"Under the canopy at the lunch terrace." The janitor hoisted a clipboard, "Have either of you been IDed yet?"

"I have," the young girl rolled up her shirtsleeve.

The man inspected the little girl's arm before he searched through the names scrawled on the pages, "Here it is; Gwen Mills, Second Grade." He scribed a note on the sheet, "Coming back into school." The janitor pointed to the stricken teenager, "What's her name?"

"Kayla something," Gwen replied.

"*Hendley,*" the bigger girl whispered in a hoarse voice, "*Kayla Hendley.*"

On the Back of the Beast

A sudden jolt signaled an immense aftershock.

The janitor careened backwards, the clipboard and papers flung haphazardly into the wind. Gwen spun around and grasped Kayla's legs, pressing the teetering teen tightly against the rattling chain link fence.

Kayla writhed in the little girl's arms and screamed with panic.

As the intense convulsions continued, Gwen shouted over and over to her terrified charge, "It's OK Kayla! IT'S OK!"

• • •

"See if you can fix that static," Gary said as he drove.

Cat reached across the dashboard of the pickup to adjust the faltering radio. They'd only been able to receive one AM station for emergency information so far.

The old truck seemed to leap into the air.

"What the..." Gary fought to regain control of the bucking vehicle.

Cat slammed sideways against the door as they slid wildly around the rubble strewn city street.

Gary spun the steering wheel to the left but the old pickup ricocheted off of several parked cars. The engine stalled and the Ford lurched to a stop in the middle of the distorted thoroughfare.

In the jittery midst of the tremor, Gary glimpsed Luis in the rear view mirror struggling to protect his comatose brother.

• • •

The runway stretched out ahead.

"I have no idea how this is going to play out," Captain Weaver told the First Officer, "the brakes might fail or the bad landing gear could buck under, so we need to be ready."

Two parallel waves puckered swiftly across the flat terrain below them.

"That's really odd;" the pilot shook his head dreamily as he watched the ground, "it's just like floating down onto a vaulting trampoline..."

"What?"

"I was just remembering Carrier Landing School. One of the flight instructors said touching down on a ship was like landing on a trampoline."

The men saw several more ripples race over the land.

On the Back of the Beast

"What's going on down there, Dick?" the pilot asked.

"The tower says to go around, they're having some sort of seismic activity. Probably aftershocks from the big earthquake."

Burt Weaver banked the massive plane for another try, "Hopefully we have enough fuel for a second attempt."

• • •

"...I think Michael's right. It doesn't make any sense to spend all this time trying to retrieve the secretary's body. We should just get out of here, Mr. Newman, before something..." Evan froze in mid-sentence.

An unexpected jolt tossed the teen sideways into a jagged pile of debris.

The wreckage of the school office groaned and squeaked oddly with the abrupt rattling. Michael let loose his end of the fallen beam and Mr. Newman briefly held the full weight of the fat timber before he foundered to the churning ground.

The three rescuers cowered amongst the wildly gyrating shards and splinters of the disintegrating building.

• • •

"...she says, don't worry baby...everything thing will turn out alright...don't worry darling..."

Oh, this really sucks, Doug thought. He couldn't remember anymore of the song that he'd been whispering to himself in the dark.

He held desperately to the topmost stair for support in the foul neck-high water.

This hunched position should be excruciating, he realized, but he felt surprisingly good in the frigid water.

Maybe the surfer songs were helping: He felt almost toasty warm.

Doug drifted off.

The brawling roar reminded him of the sea. Waves smashed over him. He slipped below the turbid swirling breakers and tumbled about in the seething turbulence.

• • •

Frank handed the binoculars back to TJ, "What do you think?"

The two men stood together in the wind at the broken edge of the pavement. Far off to the northeast, on one of the narrow roads that snaked over the hills from the Central Valley, Frank had spotted several slowly advancing sets of flashing red lights.

"Mmm," TJ lowered the binoculars. "Look! There's some more to the left." He checked the new discovery in the eyepieces. "Definitely fire trucks. It's taking them forever. I can see a guy walking in front..."

The asphalt plunged abruptly below the young man. The indispensable binoculars were catapulted downslope. TJ reached back to Frank. The older man snatched his wrist and the two toppled back onto the unruly parking lot.

Frank's head slammed hard against the oscillating ground. Everything flashed momentarily to glimmering gray before he desperately struggled back from unconsciousness.

"FRANK!" TJ pulled at his arm, "We've gotta get away from the edge!"

11. The grind at ground level

Captain Weaver realized that he was holding his breath while the damaged passenger plane slowly descended towards the runway in Sacramento. Many fire trucks poised ominously around the fringes of the landing strip awaiting their imminent contact with the pavement.

This was it, he thought.

• • •

As the smashed pickup continued slowly down Ashby Avenue towards Alviso Hospital in Berkeley, Cat Torres shook her head in disbelief. She had traveled this route many times before as a grad student on her way to the University of California. Most of the posh homes that surrounded the ravaged Claremont Hotel laid in ruins. A few residents either milled about dumbfoundedly or franticly dug through the wreckage of their former homes in search of lost loved ones. Many wailed fervently as they clustered around the dead.

The smells were frightening: smoldering structures, leaking natural gas, spilled sewage and the unmistakable scent of death.

Gary stopped the truck and pointed down the block. A huge brick apartment building had toppled, filling most of the street with an insurmountable mound of broken masonry. While many stupefied survivors clawed at the wreckage, a dusty and delirious old woman in a filthy pink bathrobe sat alone on a frayed zebra striped easy chair in the middle of the avenue. The woman's arms rose imploringly towards the heavens.

Gray backed the truck up and skirted around the brick and mortar blockage.

• • •

When the savage aftershock finally subsided, Tim sprinted out of the transmitter building in search of his companions. At the far edge of the smoke shrouded pavement he found TJ squatted over Frank who was crumpled unnaturally on the ground.

Blood spattered the surrounding asphalt from a wide gash on the back of the fallen fellow's head. The father and son wrestled the big man to a sitting position.

"This is *not* good," the injured engineer groaned. He squinted at Tim for several seconds. "I remember this sensation from dirt lot football as a kid." Frank's eyes wandered around unsynchronized. "I've got a concussion."

"It's OK Frank," TJ draped his arm over the

man's shoulder. "I bet you'll be fine in a few minutes."

Frank gasped and slumped forward, "I'm already nauseous; in a few hours, I'll be barfing all over the place." With a shaky right hand, he reached out pleadingly to Tim, "In a day I may be in a coma."

Tim studied the wounded man. "First, let's do something about that nasty mess on the back of your head." He turned to TJ, "Do we have some towels or rags in the Cherokee?"

The young man nodded.

"Go down there and get them." He turned Frank's head gently to the side and considered the bloody laceration, "We're gonna need some water too. If you can't find anything else, soak a rag with the windshield washer fluid in the plastic reservoir under the hood." Tim cleared the encrusted hair away. "It'll hurt like hell, but with the all of the alcohol and ammonia in that gunk it should work."

• • •

The strange parallax distortion seemed to cause the aircraft to remain forever suspended above the far end of the runway nearly two miles away, the Fire Chief noticed.

On the Back of the Beast

He analyzed the mangled jumbo jet as it lined up to land on Runway 34 Left at Sacramento International Airport. Since the massive earthquake in the Bay Area this morning, many aircraft had been diverted to alternative airports. Several planes were now descending upon Portland, Los Angeles or Reno, but everyone was worried about this particular Pacifica Airlines 747-8. The pilot had the great misfortune of touching down in San Francisco just as the tremor destroyed much of the landing strip. Now the crippled plane with nearly five hundred on board was about to make a risky emergency landing with major mechanical problems at *his* airport.

The Governor had called him personally to pledge any required resources and the Fire Chief had quickly assembled a significant force. The airport's six fire engines stood ready along with a dozen borrowed engines from the Sacramento Fire District and twenty-four ambulances from outlaying areas.

Now they waited for either an improbable miracle or possibly a terrible tragedy.

The plane trailed an alarming amount of smoke, he observed. At least it was nearly out of fuel, so the likelihood of a massive fire was greatly reduced.

The Fire Chief lifted the microphone, "Be ready

everyone. Stay back until the aircraft has past your location."

With the anticipated flare of bluish smoke, the sixteen rear tires struck the concrete at the far end of the runway. The jet wobbled and teetered down the landing strip.

A swirl of black smoke and the sinister orange glow of flames erupted around the left rear wheels.

"There's fire in the undercarriage!" blared from the two-way radio.

The huge plane's front landing gear dropped heavily to the earth with a violent thud. The craft drifted inexorably to the left.

"They're gonna go off the runway about halfway down," barked the Fire Chief into the microphone.

As the jet barreled towards them, it veered ponderously back and forth on the concrete before finally sliding sideways across the warning strip and skidding into the low weeds of the surrounding field.

Askew but upright, the jumbo jet came to a smoky stop off of the edge of Runway 34 Left.

"Go, Go, GO!" the Fire Chief bellowed.

On the Back of the Beast

• • •

Luis stood in the back of the idling truck pointing in frustration. The gigantic hospital loomed just six blocks away, but the streets ahead were hopelessly jammed with vehicles serving as impromptu ambulances. Dozens of badly damaged prospective patients had resorted to staggering or hobbling past the congestion to reach the Mecca of medical treatment.

The man finally bent down and pleaded with Gary through the truck's open window, "Can you help me carry Alex?"

"I guess so," Gary studied the snarled street. "I certainly don't want to get stuck in gridlock." He swung the truck around and parked halfway down a clear side street. He switched off the engine and studied the rain boots on Cat's feet. "Do you want to stay in the truck?"

The woman frowned, "I'd rather not tromp about anymore today."

"That's probably a good idea," Gary remarked. "I doubt the Emergency Room doctors would have time to clean you up for days." He handed the ignition keys to her, "Will you keep an eye on the truck? Right now, it's the only way we have of getting back to our homes."

"Sure," Cat took the ring of keys.

"Can you drive with a clutch?"

"Of course!" she laughed. "Do you think I'd drive a classic red Jaguar with an automatic?"

Gary nodded approvingly, "If any problems develop, just move a block or two and I'll find you."

He eyed several men in the distance as they looted a shattered bakery. "I think you may need a little more insurance." Gary climb out of the pickup and sorted through the odd collection of tools stored behind the bench seat. He briefly studied a stout tow chain fitted at either end with rusty metal hooks before reluctantly abandoning it. "Ah; this will do the trick." He withdrew a long and slender metal pipe with a fat black plastic handgrip.

"Is that a gun?" Cat asked in alarm.

"It looks like it," Gary laid the strange tool on the seat next to the woman. "No; it's called a powder nailer. It uses a .22 blank cartridge to drive a hardened nail into concrete."

Cat handled the heavy pseudo weapon.

"If need be, you can flash this thing around," Gary smirked, "but remember, there's no bang to back you up."

On the Back of the Beast

Cat watched Luis and Gary fumble with the unconscious teenager before they finally resorted to carrying him suspended by his arms and legs. At the end of the street, they joined the disorderly pilgrimage towards the hospital.

She locked herself in the cab of the pickup and fiddled with the radio. For some reason, the emergency broadcasts on the AM station had ceased.

• • •

After they had suffered through what was essentially a crash landing, the nearly five hundred passengers seemed remarkably calm, Captain Weaver thought as he watched them leap down the various emergency escape slides from the side of the huge plane. Apparently everyone was now certain that they'd survived the harrowing flight to Sacramento so the fear of death was no longer in play. The Fire Chief and the Airport Manager stood with him near the crashed aircraft in the open field at the edge of the runway.

"Considering all of the damage to the plane," the Fire Chief noted, "I'm amazed that you could land, let alone fly it here from San Francisco."

"I had a rougher landing once on the USS Midway. But a C-2 cargo plane is tiny compared to a 747," Burt Weaver admitted. "I could tell the aircraft was badly wrecked by the way that it

98

handled, but I had no idea of how bad."

"You know;" the Fire Chief said, "we almost never get passenger jets this size here. It looks gigantic compared to the little commuter planes that fly in and out all the time."

The Airport Manager studied the orderly rescue of the passengers. "You guys are the fourth jumbo jet diverted here today and fortunately the only one with any mechanical problems. We've got nine more big jets waiting to come in on the other runway." He shook his head, "I don't know *where* we're going to park them all. Who knows where the thousands of passengers will be spending the night."

Burt Weaver turned to the Manager, "Listen; my airline doesn't even have an office at this airport so I'm not sure how to proceed. Do you think I could go back to the Bay Area today and check on my wife?"

"Normally I'd say no," the Manager said, "you know, FAA and NTSB protocols." He laughed, "Under these strange circumstances, there won't be any investigations. I called Pacifica Headquarters and they're sending a recovery crew right now. So that's all covered."

The Airport Manager chuckled, "I don't think you realize it yet, Captain Weaver, but you are a hero now."

The Fire Chief nodded in agreement and offered his hand to the pilot, "Congratulations, sir."

"Thanks guys. I'm just glad it's over. I need to get to the terminal and find a rental car." Captain Weaver thought for a moment, "Or even better, something with four wheel drive. I really need to find Nancy."

• • •

"OW!" Frank recoiled from the windshield washer fluid soaked rag that Tim used to clean the bloody gash on his head. "Son of a bitch, that hurts!"

"It's not bleeding much anymore," Tim set aside the rag. "Let's wrap him up."

While TJ steadied the injured man, Tim wound a colorful beach towel around his head. The father and son admired the improvised bandage.

"It looks like a rainbow turban," TJ grinned.

Tim clasped his palms together and bowed his head, "We are honored by your presence, oh great maharajah."

"Yeah, yeah;" Frank groaned, "let's get back to work before I start barfing all over you two knuckleheads."

• • •

It had been at least a half an hour since Gary had left with Luis, Cat fretted.

She was crouched down on the old bench seat in the pickup peering apprehensively over the dash.

Half a block away a group of scruffy teenage boys were smashing the few remaining shop windows in the rubble-strewn business district. Ten minutes ago one of the punks had slugged an old man who had tried to stop them. The man had staggered away afterwards with his hand covering his nose, blood streamed down his face.

One of the boys hurled a brick through the big front window of a bakery. The gang roared approvingly at the defilement. They surged through the broken window.

Cat cringed when someone heaved a round cafe table into the street.

The mob pilfered voracious through the wrecked bakery.

A menacing looking teenager from the group strutted out onto the street in search of further misdeeds.

He lobbed a stone towards the pickup.

On the Back of the Beast

As she watched anxiously, Cat twisted a rumpled and bloodstained paper towel around most of the faux handgun leaving just a hint of the barrel and handgrip showing. She reached over and slipped the keys into the ignition in anticipation of a panicky escape.

The punk trotted towards the truck.

The teen stopped some distance away, a wicked grin stretched across his face.

He'd spotted her.

He withdrew a long metal object from its sheath. After three bounding steps he slammed against the truck's door.

"HEY, old lady!"

The man jerked his head to the side; the glint of the big knife clenched in his hand suggested that he was willing to use it. "GET OUT!"

Cat locked her eyes onto his and slowly raised the mock firearm into view. "BACK OFF!" she growled.

The pack of teenagers howled and bayed at the embolden attacker.

The tense deadlock between the woman and the young thug was broken when a beer bottle shattered on the pavement in front of the truck.

Cat glanced in the rearview mirror just as Gary flung a second bottle towards the teen from halfway down the street. The container crashed at the punk's feet. He sneered and raised his middle finger before he retreated back to the pack at the bakery.

Gary vaulted to the pickup truck.

Cat popped open the door and he leapt in.

"Let's get out of here!"

He revved the engine and jammed the truck into reverse, shooting them backwards past the shattered storefronts.

They stopped a few blocks away.

"Are you OK?"

Cat nodded and finally relaxed a bit, "Thanks."

Gary gripped the grimy steering wheel; "I left Luis and his brother in a long line at the Emergency Room. I don't think the kid's going to make it."

She studied him as he stared dolefully out at the devastation.

"It's been a tough day," Cat sighed. "Let's head back to where we belong."

After several seconds of gloomy introspection, Gary turned the truck towards the flatlands of west Berkeley, "I've got one more thing to check on."

12. Relief in small ways

"This should be the place," Gary pressed his brow in consternation as he stood on the fractured pavement.

"Are you sure?" Cat scrutinized the wide swath of mangled debris that covered most of one side of Harman Street, "I can't tell where one building ends and another begins."

A straggly man approached them, "Can you guys spare any food?"

Cat shook her head and the man frowned.

"Wait a minute;" Gary offered a friendly smile, "I might be able to help you out."

The man bowed slightly in appreciation of the offer.

As Gary rummaged through his pockets, he questioned the man, "Are you from this area?"

"Yeah," the man vacillated, "well, sorta; I lived in a garden shed down the street." He contemplated the havoc of fallen buildings, "At least I did before this morning."

"So you know what's going on around here,

right?" Gary produced a five-dollar bill from his pocket.

The man nodded as he eyed the rumpled banknote, "What do you want to know?"

"Which building was Harmon Welding?"

"That's it there."

"I thought so," Gary tilted his head, "I'm looking for a tall, husky guy who worked there. He's about my age with shoulder length brown hair."

"I know the guy. He's one of the welders."

"Excellent," Gary patiently smoothed the bill between his fingers. "Did you see him after the earthquake?"

"I'm pretty sure I saw him from way down the street." The man stroked his unshaven face, "There was someone who looked just like him digging around here for awhile. Then he just left."

"Thanks." Gary presented the money to the now truly homeless man. "Good luck."

Cat watched the vagrant wander off with his bounty. "I'm not particularly convinced that your brother-in-law escaped uninjured."

"I'm not either." Gary stared at the jagged brick rubble. "It would have been tough to make it out alive when the building collapsed. But he could have been outside when it hit. I guess I'll find out eventually one way or the other."

He walked slowly back to the pickup with the disheveled woman. "Let's see if we can get over the hills."

• • •

"You're back," the woman at the triage area said to Gwen in a less-than-friendly tone.

"Mr. Newman asked me to bring this kid over here from the high school," the little girl told the dour adult.

The woman's eyebrows arched up, "I hear it's really bad over there." She prodded Kayla's swollen arm.

The teenager yelped.

Gwen nodded, "The whole school was flattened. There's a bunch of people over there trying to find survivors." The little girl smiled victoriously, "I discovered Kayla buried in the school office."

"Kayla;" the woman wrote the name at the bottom of a long list of patients. "What's Kayla's last name?"

On the Back of the Beast

"Hendley," the teenager said weakly.

"And your grade level, Miss Hendley?" The woman opened a large medicine bottle.

"Twelfth."

"Take these two Tylenols. You're not going to die from that arm injury." The woman ran her fingers carefully along the swollen skin, "But someone should x-ray it for breaks." She thought for a moment, "I'll put you down as a three."

Gwen twisted her head quizzically, "Three?"

The woman wrote a note next to Kayla's name, "Non life threatening injury that requires some medical attention." The woman set the paperwork aside and uncapped a black laundry marker, "Normally I'd put this on your left arm, but we'll have to use your right."

"For what?" Kayla asked.

"Look," Gwen rolled up her left shirtsleeve to reveal carefully lettered identification information. "I got this earlier before they would let me go over to the high school with Mr. Newman."

Kayla examined the girl's arm, "Gwen Mills. What does the '2 LGS 5' mean?"

"Second Grade at Lincoln Grade School," Gwen said proudly. "I think the five means that I'm uninjured."

The groggy teen turned to the woman, "Why are you writing on everyone's arms?"

"There's a few people in here," the woman sighed sadly, "that will hopefully be taken over to the hospital sometime today." She pointed to the ghastly looking group at the far edge of the lunch terrace. "They're the number ones and a few of the badly injured number twos. Most of them can't talk. We want the doctors, and if need be, the coroner to be able to identify them. So that's why we're writing identifying information on everyone."

Gwen rubbed at the ink on her arm, "Is this permanent like a tattoo? Because I've always wanted one."

"It'll wear off in a few days." The woman finished her work on the stricken teenager. "*Don't* leave this area without telling someone. We've already lost three kids who apparently snuck out of here."

Gwen studied the black markings on the teen's arm: 'Kayla Hendley, 12 JHS 3.'

"Alright ladies," the woman finally smiled at the girls, "threes through fives need to wait over there. They tell me that someone is going to serve some food in about ten minutes."

Gwen helped Kayla to stand and they ventured into the subdued assemblage of injured students.

The youngster glanced up at the teenager as she led her along by the hand, "I was wondering about something, maybe you can help me figure it out."

The two girls selected an unoccupied spot at one of the many green metal picnic benches of the crowded Lunch Terrace-cum-Triage Area.

"I'll try;" Kayla replied anemically, "but I'm not very smart."

"What's a coroner?" the little girl asked.

• • •

"You're worried about your brother-in-law," Cat finally said. The long and slow trip up the winding and mutilated road had been completely devoid of conversation.

"Yeah;" Gary admitted, "him and my daughter. Although for some reason, I think she's probably just fine."

He edged the truck gently around a crushed

110

BMW that protruded from a rockslide. "They were both sitting next to me on the bench seat of the truck just a few hours ago."

"Wow!" Cat exclaimed, "It's really smoky up here."

Gary nodded, "Hopefully we won't have to back track."

"You're only worried about those two?" Cat asked.

"I guess my neighbors too," Gary admitted. "Flint and Reesa. They're a retired couple." He chuckled, "Those two are always together."

"Flint and Reesa;" Cat repeated, "Great names. What's your daughter's name?"

"Kayla. Kayla Marie Hendley."

Cat dithered for several seconds before she finally asked the sensitive question, "What about Kayla Marie Hendley's mom?"

"I'm sure she's fine," Gary laughed. "We haven't seen her in years. She lives with husband number three somewhere in New Jersey. Kayla's got two stepsisters that she's never even met."

"Sorry."

"It's alright;" Gary glanced at her and smiled, "her mom and I were both young and stupid at the time. What about you? Is there a Mr. Torres?"

"My Dad, but he's been dead for years," she snorted. "I never really had the time for that whole marriage and babies thing."

The truck rounded a sharp corner and skidded to a stop. They had reached the rugged top of the Oakland/Berkeley Hills.

"Unbelievable," Cat uttered as she watched the distant and disturbing spectacle.

Across a wide canyon, a huge wildfire ate away at the profuse dry vegetation of early fall. Even from nearly three miles away, they could feel the intense wavering heat of the massive firestorm.

"That's near the mansion," Gary noted.

Cat watched the gusty ridge top winds whip the towering flames into several incandescent tornados.

"*I would have been burned to death*," she whispered.

Gary rubbed her shoulder sympathetically. "I suspect many others were, Ms Torres."

• • •

The little girl giggled mischievously.

"I don't think that my Mom would approve of this meal," Gwen jammed a third chocolate bar into her mouth, "but it's really good."

After several minutes of rest on the green picnic bench and a snack of candy bars, Gatorade and stale corn chips, Kayla felt much better. She grinned as she watched her amusing young companion gulp the light blue beverage from an oversized container.

Gwen brushed at the blue liquid that dribbled from her overstuffed mouth and smeared a long streak of melted chocolate across her cheek in the process.

"You are a mess, young lady!" Kayla scolded mockingly. "Hold still." The teenager dabbed at the little girl's face.

The frivolity was interrupted by the painful shriek of a little boy from the other end of the Triage Area.

Gwen set down the beverage container and tilted her head in concern, "I know that kid." She stood up on the bench for a better view of the wailing child, "It's one of the First Grade boys." Gwen slowly sat down with a look of deep distress. "His name is Jackson. Sometimes we play together."

113

On the Back of the Beast

Several adults clustered around the screaming child.

"I hope he's OK," Gwen grimaced.

Kayla stroked the youngster's taut shoulders. The girl seemed especially affected by the painful drama. "Ah;" Kayla struggled to find some sort of distraction, "thanks for saving me."

Gwen brow furrowed as she watched the adults tend to the injured boy.

"Hey;" the teenager twisted the youngster around to face her, "that pink helmet that you were wearing; it was so funny that it kept slipping over your eyes."

"Yeah;" Gwen glanced back to the wounded boy, "Mr. Newman found it when we first started digging around at the high school." She had a faraway look of concentration as she remembered the earlier events of the chaotic day. "I think he was worried that I'd get hurt."

"I'm glad you didn't."

"It was fun searching around," Gwen finally smiled, "I was pretending to hunt for treasure in a secret dark cave when I found you." She stopped for a moment, "How come you were in the office? Did you get in trouble?"

Kayla flinched at the question. Her eyes slowly

114

teared up as she remembered the agonizing events of the morning.

Gwen studied the sad teen.

"They were going to kick me out of school," Kayla finally whispered.

"Did you get in a fight or steal someone's lunch?" Gwen asked.

"No. It's because I'm stupid and I got bad grades."

Tears streamed down the teen's ashen face.

"You sound like my little brother when you whine." Gwen frowned, "That's the second time that you said you weren't very smart." With a stern look of disapproval, she lectured the weepy teenager, "Crying about your problems isn't going to help. You need to try harder."

"But I'm never gonna graduate from Jefferson High School," Kayla moaned.

"Who cares!" The little girl laughed unexpectedly, "The school was destroyed by an earthquake! Nobody's going to graduate from that place."

The high school student slowly nodded as she considered the Second Grader's keen observation. "You're right."

13. The intimate sense of disaster

"Good news, guys!" TJ announced as he returned to the transmitter building. "Frank was right about the backup generator. It started right up as soon as I pressed the reset button."

"The power came back on in here about five minutes ago," Tim noted as he configured the computer program. "We should be back on the air shortly."

TJ squatted over Frank who was stretched out on the floor in the small room, "How are you feeling?"

"D...dizzy." the man stammered. "I gotta keep my eyes closed...or I'll vomit."

Tim activated the microphone, "This is AM 600 and we are back on the air after a particularly nasty aftershock at about 12:30 PM. Our own Frank Johnson was injured during the tremor and we believe that he has suffered a concussion. Hopefully, we can evacuate him to a hospital in the near future."

The ailing engineer retched.

• • •

"OK; now it's your turn," Kayla said as they merrily entertained each other in the otherwise grim Triage Area.

"Mmm; let me think," Gwen tapped her head in concentration, "my five favorite things." A broad smile lit her face, "Well; I *just* did a report about it: playing on the monkey bars, camping, reading and kittens."

"I love kittens too," Kayla crooned. "My neighbor's cat just had babies and they're *so* cute!"

"Wait;" Gwen counted to herself, "that was only four things." She thought for a minute. "My number one favorite thing now is chocolate and Gatorade for lunch."

"Chocolate," the teenager nodded. "I'm still hungry, I wonder if there's any left?"

"Me too." The youngster surveyed the dreary Lunch Terrace. "I'll be right back. I'm going to try to find something for us to eat."

Kayla watched the happy-go-lucky girl skip away on her quest for surplus candy.

• • •

TJ realized that he spent most of the time now at the windy corner of the blacktop as he watched

117

the procession of Emergency vehicles creep along on the road far below.

He certainly did not like to see Frank suffer and the smell of vomit in the stuffy transmitter room had nearly made him sick too. His dad had managed to tend to the ailing man and continue to broadcast information about the crisis. With Frank puking every five minutes, how were they going to get out of here?

TJ's eyes watered from the swirling black smoke that blustered erratically across the peak. He'd better get back and report on the advancing fire trucks.

• • •

"Hi Kayla," a deep male voice interrupted her daydream.

"Oh," the teenager stared blankly at the disheveled man. "You were with Gwen when I was rescued."

"I'm Mr. Newman, one of the Fourth Grade teachers here." He inspected her swollen arm, "How are you feeling now?"

"*Way* better than before."

"I'll bet." The teacher had a strange look of trepidation. "Where is Gwen?"
118

"She'll be right back." Kayla smirked, "She's trying to find some chocolate for us."

"Mmm; I've got some bad news." Mr. Newman hunched down and whispered, "They just found her little brother, Rowan, in the wreckage of the Kindergarten classroom and he's in terrible shape."

"Is he going to die?"

"I...I'm not..," the man faltered. "They don't think he'll make it. His injuries are quite severe. The poor little guy was buried for hours..."

"That's terrible," Kayla frowned. "Gwen's such a good kid."

"I know," the teacher slumped sadly. "Many people have died today. Dozens at this school and hundreds across the street at the high school. Probably thousands in the whole Bay Area."

Mr. Newman added gloomily, "Everyone will end up being affected by this earthquake in some tragic way. We're all going to have to take good care of each other."

"I had no idea," Kayla contemplated the demoralizing assessment.

"Rowan may pull through," the man added, "but if he doesn't, Gwen will need plenty of compassionate attention." He stood and offered her a look of sad resignation, "Three of my own students were killed this morning and I guess I felt that if we could save some victims, maybe that would help me cope with their deaths later."

"I'll be around if you two need anything," the weary man left the teen to her own thoughts.

• • •

Kayla watched the little girl wend her way around the picnic benches crowded with her bandaged and bruised schoolmates. She had a particularly intense and doleful look. Perhaps Gwen already knew about her brother's condition.

Try to be cheerful, Kayla told herself.

"Did you find anything to eat?"

"Two candy bars," Gwen reported woefully.

"Two is good," Kayla took a deep breath and ventured forward. "Why are you so sad?"

"I think that I'm more worried than sad," the girl tipped her head in thought.

"About what?"

"I found these candy bars and I was hunting

around for a few more. I ended up over by the number one kids," the youngster reported.

"Number one kids?" Kayla asked.

"The guys that got really badly hurt."

Kayla nodded.

"I saw a girl who's in my brother's Kindergarten class. She was sitting on top of one of the picnic tables. She was really dirty and covered with dried blood," Gwen pressed her eyes closed as she recalled the troubling incident.

Kayla wrapped her right arm around the little girl's waist.

"The kid kept shivering like she was really cold. She was holding on to something that was laying on the table, but I couldn't see what it was."

A miserable and faraway look settled on her face, "Some adults came over to the Kindergartner and pried her hand loose; and that's when I realized that it was another kid."

"So there were two of them together?"

Gwen nodded, "The girl was holding on to the hand of a dead kid."

Kayla frowned, "That's *so* sad."

"One of the adults carried the body away. The little Kindergarten girl just kept shaking, I don't think that she even knew that her friend was gone." Gwen nestled on the bench next to the teenager, "Both of those kids are in my brother's class. That's when I realized that I haven't seen Rowan since this morning."

Kayla kissed Gwen's straggly hair. She was at a loss as to how to proceed, should she tell the little girl what she knew of Rowan or just hope for a happy conclusion?

"I've been thinking about my Dad and my Uncle Doug," Kayla finally said, "hopefully, they'll come and get me soon."

"I'm worried about my Mom and Dad too," Gwen admitted. "What happens if nobody comes for us?"

"I don't know. Maybe we can ask Mr. Newman."

• • •

This was the most bizarre traffic jam that he'd ever seen, Captain Weaver thought.

He edged the rented SUV forward behind the large sluggish vehicle. The Fire Chief at the Sacramento airport had suggested this route back to Alamo, assuring him that the roads were passable. He certainly felt safe on the
122

overcrowded road.

The rented SUV inched along the rural road at three miles per hour in the middle of a huge ragtag convoy of emergency vehicles.

• • •

"Hey, Mr. Newman," Gwen greeted the sullen teacher as he checked on various students in the Triage Area.

"Hi Gwen," the man offered a halfhearted smile, "how's my favorite Second Grader?"

"Pretty good," the little girl thought for a moment, "but kinda hungry."

Kayla nodded in agreement.

"I was wondering about some stuff," the youngster said.

Mr. Newman's eyebrows arched apprehensively.

"What happens if nobody comes here to get a kid?"

"That's a good question," the teacher said. "We discussed that very thing at a teacher's meeting in September." He sat wearily on the bench next to Kayla. "Officially, after three days we're supposed turn over any students who don't get picked up to the county protective services."

"County protective what?" Gwen asked.

"Like foster care?" Kayla cringed. "That would really suck."

"It's a government agency that takes care of children if their parents are unable to do it." The man looked around at the multitude of students at the Lunch Terrace who were waiting for someone to retrieve them. "I suspect that we will end up just sending kids home with friends if a relative doesn't come for them tonight."

Gwen thought for several minutes about that disquieting possibility. "I've got another question, Mr. Newman."

"What is it?"

"Have you seen my little brother?"

Mr. Newman frowned and Kayla shuddered.

Gwen's eyes narrowed at the reaction that her question had provoked, "Did something happen to Rowan?"

The teenager pressed her eyes shut and whimpered.

"I know where he is, Gwen," the teacher finally admitted.

The girl anxiously surveyed the benches for her brother, "He's not around here. I know that for sure."

Kayla gazed teary-eyed at Mr. Newman, "I think you should tell her."

"Yeah;" the man vacillated, "you're right." He took a long slow breath before he continued, "When we searched around at the high school after the earthquake, we looked for two people." He placed a trembling hand on the teenager's shoulder, "We were lucky enough to rescue Kayla; but sadly, the school secretary didn't survive the collapse of the office."

Gwen's face rippled with dread.

The girl steadied herself and stared up at the teacher, "Did Rowan die?"

"I'm afraid so."

14. Fortune/Misfortune

The long thin shadows of early evening stretched across the flat black expanse of asphalt on the top of the mountain. On any other day, TJ realized, he would have especially enjoyed the gorgeous ruby sunset. But the turbulently whirling smoke and the daunting implications from the two monstrous fires deterred any pleasure.

They had no food or water. Sleeping on the gusty peak would be trying even in the best conditions. Frank Johnson was getting sicker by the hour. Their Jeep was wrecked.

His dad had taken a break from the toil of broadcasting and tending to the ill man to seek him out. The father and son had reluctantly agreed that they would hike down the rugged path in the morning carrying Frank in a homemade stretcher. Difficult as it seemed, the arduous trek appeared to be their only option.

• • •

"I *do* live up there," Captain Weaver pointed towards the hill as he spoke to the skeptical policeman though the open window of the rented SUV, "in James Bowie Court."

"James Bowie Court, huh?" The surly officer shone his flashlight through the interior of the vehicle. "I'll need to see some identification."

"Here you go," Burt forced a pleasant grin as he presented his driver's license to the man.

The policeman carefully examined the document. "Alright, you can go up there. But I must warn you that Law Enforcement has been authorized to use whatever force that is necessary to stop looting."

"I understand."

The officer passed the license back to Captain Weaver, "You must return to this location within two hours or face arrest."

"I will."

"There's not much left up there." The man's demeanor softened, "good luck."

• • •

On the outskirts of Lafayette, Cat and Gary encountered a turbulent new river that had chewed an erratic ravine through the road into town. The woman speculated that the torrent had likely originated from the reservoir situated in the surrounding hills.

Gary skirted around the obstruction by diverting onto Upper Happy Valley Road. They wended their way past the mostly intact Bentley High School and dozens of flattened homes before they returned to the main thoroughfare.

"I hate to say it," he told her as they bumped along the dark and squalid road, "but we're almost out of gas."

"With the power being out and all of the destruction," Cat noted, "I doubt that we'll find an open station anytime soon."

Gary gawked at the smashed storefronts and gutted restaurants sprinkled around the fringe of the well-to-do town. "I'm surprised at how *few* people we've seen since we left Berkeley."

"You're right," Cat concurred. "I guess the earthquake trapped many people in fallen buildings."

Near the center of Lafayette, the pickup edged around several fire trucks that clogged the main street. Gary stopped and they watched the exhausted firefighters mop up the scattered incandescent remnants of a titanic inferno that had destroyed most of the downtown.

"Almost all of my choice hangouts were in this area," the woman lamented.

• • •

Gwen had pressed herself into a sad little ball as she nestled under Kayla's good arm. The teenager had been trying her best to comfort the miserable little girl.

"Now I know how the Kindergartner felt," the youngster confided.

"What Kindergartner?" Kayla asked her despondent companion.

"The kid who was holding on to her dead friend." Gwen shook her head plaintively, "I just *can't* believe that he's gone."

Kayla closed her eyes and gently stroked the girl's wispy hair.

The little girl quivered a bit, "If Rowan died in the earthquake, maybe my Mom and Dad were killed too."

The teenager cringed at the suggestion, "Shhhh; everything is going to be alright."

"*No;*" Gwen murmured, "*it's too late for that.*"

• • •

Burt Weaver painstakingly traveled along the residential streets that he had absentmindedly traveled thousands of times in the past. A wide strip of perhaps twenty swanky mansions had been reduced to merely great billowing silver mounds of hot fly ash. The formerly regal houses were wantonly supplanted by lowly gray foundation walls and a few sturdy stone embellishments.

He turned left onto a narrow street. The firestorm had spared his neighborhood. The headlights darted across many low ranch homes but not a single one was undamaged. Burt ventured into the long windy cul-de-sac that contained his house. He drove slowly past the flattened suburban residences. Several exhausted acquaintances scavenging through their decimated dwellings stared blankly at the unfamiliar vehicle that skulked along the littered roadway.

Parked in front of his shattered house was Nancy's silver Lexus, the silhouette of his dozing wife was clearly visible in the driver's seat.

"Oh, thank God," he blurted. Captain Weaver parked the rented SUV and sprinted to the sedan.

Nancy pushed open the door and euphorically wrapped her arms around his waist. "I'm so glad your back!"

The two clung together in a long and weepy embrace.

She finally loosened her hold on him, "Let's sit in the car and get out of the sooty air."

Burt joined her in the Lexus. "Where were you when it happened?"

She smiled at him with glistening eyes, "I was just pulling out of the parking lot at the market. Everything bounced around and I nearly plowed into another car. But I just held on to the steering wheel for dear life."

"The car seems to be OK," Burt checked around the auto.

Nancy nodded. "I drove up here afterwards. I helped Lisa and Eric down the street collect a few mementos before they left for their daughter's house in Santa Cruz."

"What about the fires?" he asked.

"We could see all of the smoke. A man drove by and suggested that we leave, but I wanted to stay here until I absolutely had to flee, just in case you came back." She leaned across the seat and kissed his cheek.

"Our house is a mess," he observed. "Have you been inside, dear?"

131

"No, I've been too afraid to go into it. During one of the aftershocks, the chimney came tumbling down." She caressed his hand, "Were you in the air during the earthquake, darling?"

"We were landing," Burt stiffened as he recalled the harrowing incident. "The plane was damaged but Dick and I diverted to Sacramento. We touched down at around one in the afternoon and I've been driving since then."

"I bet you're starved."

"Yes I am," he admitted.

"Can I offer you a ham sandwich?" she suggested. "All I have is raisin bread, but I had one earlier and it was surprisingly good."

"Really? A ham sandwich?" he asked incredulously.

"The groceries that I bought this morning are still in the trunk," she smiled. "I was going to make you a nice steak for dinner tonight, but that doesn't seem likely now."

Burt devoured the unorthodox sandwich that she prepared for him.

Nancy snuggled next to him in the back seat, "I bought a nice bottle of wine for dinner but I can't figure out how to open it without a corkscrew."

• • •

The helicopter arched slowly overhead. The long metal rotors blades whacked deafeningly at the smoldery evening air. Tim and TJ watched the loitering craft with interest from the doorway of the transmitter building.

"Do you think they're going to land?" the younger man asked.

"I hope so."

The noisy machine descended to the blacktop. The door of the clamorous craft opened and a helmet-clad middle-aged man bound out and ran towards them. With a wide grin, he joined the men at the transmitter building.

"Lloyd Gozport! Son of a bitch; what are you doing here?" Tim asked in amazement.

"Ah; Mr. O'Keefe, I heard there was a minor problem at my transmitter site," he teased.

TJ brushed the fluttering hair from his face, "We are really glad to see you, sir!"

Four men scurried out of the idling helicopter. While three of the new arrivals unloaded several boxes, the fourth man recorded the hectic work with a large video camera.

"Don't get me wrong," Tim shook his head as he watched the busy men, "it's a pleasure to see you, Mr. Gozport. But this little stunt must be costing you a fortune."

"Are you kidding?" Lloyd smiled. "You guys are heroes! The Mighty AM 600 has been the only radio station operating consistently during the crises. The Governor figures that all of those reports that you put out about the fires probably saved ten thousand lives. You can't buy publicity like that!"

"What's in the boxes?" TJ asked.

"Supplies for the Radio Engineers and the camera crew," Lloyd said smugly. "I told them to keep the transmitter operating and to continue to send out reports. They're going to beam some video of the fires out for the networks in the next hour or so."

"I'd hate to break up the show, boss," Tim said, "but we have a badly injured man inside the transmitter building."

"We're way ahead of you. The Emergency Room Doctors at Sacramento Memorial Hospital are waiting for Mr. Johnson's arrival."

Tim O'Keefe smiled appreciatively, "Apparently the Marines have come to our rescue."

TJ and Lloyd helped Frank into the helicopter while Tim briefly explained the process of building the makeshift radio station to the engineers. The cameraman followed along with the TV camera. Lloyd Gozport would make sure that this would all end up being broadcasted endlessly during the next few days, he mused.

The exhausted Transmitter Site Supervisor joined the others in the helicopter.

Tim peered out of the small side window as the craft slowly rose from the mountaintop. The engineers waved from the open door of the transmitter building and the cameraman tilted the TV camera up to document the departure of the audacious but reluctant radiomen.

The tough old Irishman was momentarily overcome by an intense sense of relief.

• • •

Cat shook her head in disbelief as they drove slowly down the country road towards her mansion. The lingering heat from the recent conflagration was nearly unbearable. Tire tracks left by previous travelers rutted the flame-soften asphalt. Smoke billowed relentlessly across the scorched terrain. A thick black cloud momentarily engulfed the pickup.

"Fire has not been my friend today," the woman bleakly noted.

"Where exactly are we going?" Gary squinted into the gloom.

"This is my driveway, turn left here."

They journeyed down the long drive. Cat pressed her hand over her mouth in shock. Her fanciful chateau had vanished. Three stalwart chimneys, the distorted metal skeletons of nearly a dozen charred cars and a lone concrete sidewall of the garage were all that remained of her once grand manor.

Gary turned the truck slowly around the property to direct the headlights across the destruction.

"I *did* design it to withstand an substantial earthquake but I don't think anything could have survived a giant wildfire," Cat moaned.

"Hopefully my housekeeper and mechanic escaped."

They sat silently in the truck cab. Gary patiently endured the somber funeral-like finality of the lifeless landscape and Cat lamented the loss of her extravagant home and lifestyle.

"I have nowhere to go," the woman finally declared.

136

Gary sighed heavily, he kept getting tangled up in other people's problems when all he wanted to do was to find Kayla and return to his own home. "Why don't you come with me?"

Cat shrugged, "What choice do I have?"

15. The forsaken

"What a mess!" Cat examined the shambles of the fallen high school in the dim evening light.

Gary stood stunned next to her at the entrance to Jefferson High School.

She turned to him, "There doesn't seem to be anyone here. What should we do?"

"I don't know," he slowly shook his head. "All that I've thought about since the earthquake this morning was that I had to get back to here to pick up Kayla. It didn't even occur to me that I might not be able to find her."

"Let's look around," Cat said, "maybe we'll find somebody who knows what's going on."

Gary nodded.

They picked their way past the rubble-strewn entrance and eventually ended up at the flattened school office. Cat stopped to consider a dead woman splayed out under a stout timber, "This is number three."

Gary stared quizzically at her, "What?"

"I'd never seen a dead person before the earthquake," Cat reflected, "this unfortunate lady is the third one that I've come upon today."

He studied the corpse for several seconds, "I suppose someone is probably wondering and worrying about what has become of her."

Cat nodded, "I suspect that thousands of people all around the Bay Area are being tortured right now with that horrible sense of uncertainty and dread."

They wandered on.

"Look!" Gary glanced past her; "I see some light over there."

The feeble and erratic beam from a flashlight flitted in the distance.

"Let's find out what that's all about."

They soon discovered several rescuers searching for survivors in the ruins of the Girl's Locker Room. A bleary-eyed man directed Gary and Cat across the street to Lincoln Grade School where many of the remaining students were waiting.

• • •

"Please?" Kayla asked. "Please just have a little bit of the chocolate with me, Gwen?"

The melancholy child studied the offering.

139

On the Back of the Beast

"You'll feel better if you eat something," Kayla said hopefully.

Gwen nibbled timidly on the candy.

She stopped in mid bite and pointed to Mr. Newman as he led two weary adults into the Triage Area, "It looks like someone is getting picked up," the youngster sulked, "but it's not going to be me."

Kayla sat up and studied the approaching adults, "That's my Dad!" She wobbled to her feet.

The man grinned in recognition and sprinted towards them.

"WATCH THE ARM!" Kayla dodged her father while she clinched her damaged appendage tightly to her chest.

Gary stopped short and stared at his long-lost daughter, "I'm so glad to see you!"

Kayla pressed against her father's side as she wept at her fortunate redemption.

Mr. Newman and the woman joined the group at the bench. Many of the forlorn students on the Lunch Terrace watched the reunion enviously. The teacher turned to the rain boot-clad woman, "Are you Kayla's mom?"

"No;" Cat shook her head, "I guess you could say that Gary and I used to work together. It seems so long ago," she had a faraway look of reminiscence, "but I guess it was just this morning."

Kayla kissed her father's cheek, "Dad; this is Gwen. She and Mr. Newman found me in the school office. They dug me out of a huge pile of junk."

"Thank you," Gary bowed slightly to the man and the little girl.

"Who's the woman?" Kayla asked. "Where's Uncle Doug?"

Gary glanced furtively at Cat, "I'm not sure where Doug is right now."

Cat intervened with a warm smile, "Hi Kayla, I'm Catalina Torres. Your dad was kind enough to give me a ride from Oakland after my car was totaled in the earthquake."

Kayla examined the woman for several seconds.

"Cat is going to stay with us for awhile," Gary said. "Her house burned down and she has no place to live now."

"Sure;" Kayla shrugged, "I don't have any problem with that."

On the Back of the Beast

Gwen stood downcast next to the green bench as she watched the reunion. Mr. Newman placed his big hand protectively on the little girl's sagging shoulders.

"We should be going." Gary motioned towards the exit, "I have no idea what our house looks like now."

Mr. Newman smiled, "You'll need to sign Kayla out."

The teacher led the group to the check-out table. "I need your signature here. Obviously, she needs some medical attention in the near future..."

While her father and Mr. Newman completed the paperwork, Kayla watched Gwen slump on the green metal bench by herself. Her hapless little heroine would now have to suffer alone.

The teenager blinked back the stinging in her eyes. The rescuer needed to be rescued.

"Wait."

The men stopped their work.

Kayla shook her head, "This just isn't right."

Gary looked at his daughter in alarm, "Is your arm bothering you?"

142

"No;" Kayla said with consternation, "I can't leave Gwen here!"

She spun around and stared pleadingly at her father. "She saved my life and took good care of me." Kayla's voice cracked with emotion, "She's really worried about being left behind." Kayla pressed her eyes shut, "Her brother just died and I don't think she'll be able to deal with that by herself."

"It's OK, Kayla," Gary cooed to his daughter, "I'm sure her parents will be here soon."

"I don't think so," Mr. Newman slowly shook his head, "they both work in Oakland and I heard it's pretty bad over there."

Cat nodded, "It's really bad everywhere."

Gary sighed wearily, "Well; what can we do?"

"Dad, we have to take care of Gwen," Kayla told her reluctant father. "She's just a little kid and I think she's really scared right now."

Mr. Newman's eyebrows arched up, "It would make a gigantic difference in her life if someone took the time to help her though this trying situation."

"OK;" Gary finally relented, "she can stay with us until someone comes for her."

On the Back of the Beast

Kayla broke free from her father and returned to the youngster on the green bench.

The adults watched the seventeen-year-old retrieve the forsaken child.

The teacher smiled, "There's a little more paperwork to do, I guess." He studied the names on the long roster, "Here next to Gwen's name; write down the address where you will be staying and at least two different telephone numbers where we can get a hold of you when her parents finally arrive. Although I doubt we'll have phone service anytime soon. We can't seem to get any cell phone signals and I think most of the land lines are out too."

The two girls joined the adults at the table.

"Thank you *so* much." Gary shook the teacher's hand. "Maybe you can help me with a little problem?"

"I'll try," Mr. Newman replied.

"My truck is completely out of gas," Gary confessed.

"I can't help you with that but I do know someone who can."

• • •

144

The bedraggled foursome traveled slowly across the darkened school parking lot. Cat Torres lead the girls towards the parked truck. Gwen gently guided Kayla by the hand as the teen plodded achingly forward. Gary lugged a wash bucket filled with gasoline that he and the head janitor had drained from a wrecked car in the teacher's lot.

"You have to get in on the driver's side," Gary directed his daughter when she approached the bashed passenger door of the old pickup.

Kayla cradled her inflamed arm against her chest, "What happened to the truck?"

Gary carefully emptied the gas into a borrowed funnel that protruded from the pickup's tank, "We had a little trouble in Berkeley during one of the aftershocks."

Gwen ran her fingers over the crumpled door, "Were you playing bumper cars?"

"Not intentionally," Cat smiled at the youngster.

Gary placed the bucket and funnel in the truck's bed and meandered around to the front of the vehicle. He held open the driver's door and Cat slid across the seat to the far side. The little girl studied the interior of the worn out truck.

"Since I saved her life," Gwen told Gary with

great sincerity, "I should sit next to Kayla."

Cat stifled a chuckle as she watched the pint-sized heroine declare her wishes to the dispassionate man.

Gary nodded to the plucky girl, "Fair enough."

16. The lost and the found

Without the usual infrequently spaced streetlights, the twisting rural road seemed especially treacherous. The battered pickup crept leerily along the smoke-shrouded roadway.

The four exhausted travelers stoically endured the slow journey.

Gary clung to the grimy steering wheel and squinted vigilantly out at the broken pavement. He had already stopped twice in the short half mile from the main road to move boulders and tree branches aside. Cat sat pressed against the passenger's door and stared pensively out of the window. Gwen was wedged next to the woman, jerking and fidgeting in and out of an uneasy slumber. The little girl was no doubt suffering through the shock of her brother's death. Kayla quivered and groaned with every painful bounce and jolt. Her throbbing arm was now mottled and bruised.

The truck jarred to a stop. In the headlights ahead were the shadowy remains of a huge fallen oak. The tree had apparently been pushed onto the roadway by a giant rockslide. Dangling from dozens of kinked and twisted limbs were flitting ribbons of aluminum foil.

The strips twinkled and shimmered weirdly in the stark smoky light from the truck.

"It's beautiful," the drowsy little girl commented.

Cat tipped her head to consider the unexpected spectacle, "It is, isn't it?" A funny little half smile darted across her smudged face.

Kayla momentarily forgot about her injured arm, "This must have taken hours."

"It looks like something that Flint would do to warn unwary drivers," Gary said.

"Who's Flint?" Gwen asked Kayla.

"Our next door neighbor," the teenager studied the elaborate display. "He and Reesa are almost like grandparents to me."

"Oh." Gwen thought for a moment, "Didn't you say they have kittens?"

Kayla nodded.

A long trail of hand painted white arrows on the roadway seemed to beckon the travelers around the obstacle. Gary swung the truck to the right and ventured into an adjoining field to bypass the blockage.

148

A few minutes after returning to the pavement, they turned onto a long and narrow common driveway. Part way down the drive, they stopped at a house with a cheery little campfire that burned in an improvised pit on the front lawn. An elderly couple waved from the sanctuary of two lawn chairs piled high with quilts and comforters.

A scruffy old man slid out from under the warm mound and approached the vehicle, "Gary! Damn good to see you!"

"Hey Flint; how are you two holding up?"

"Not bad, considering everything."

A small and gray woman joined him. She eyed the strange group of riders. "Who's that with you?"

"Adversity brings together peculiar traveling companions." Gary introduced the little girl, "Reesa and Flint; this is Gwen. She rescued Kayla from the wreckage of the school office."

The youngster beamed at the recounting of her heroic deed.

"We're going to look after Gwen until her folks show up." He pointed to the woman at the opposite end of the long bench seat, "That's Cat Torres. She's the architect for the house that I was working on. Her place in Lafayette was

149

destroyed by fire, so she's going to stay with us for awhile."

Flint and Reesa exchanged a look of surprise.

"Are you guys hungry?" Flint asked. "We've got a huge pot of baked beans bubbling away on the fire. We've already fed some of the other neighbors who've stopped by."

Gary surveyed the travelers in the truck, "What do you think?"

Everyone nodded affirmatively.

They clustered around the fire pit to eat and retell their various stories of survival.

Flint ladled great mounds of steaming beans onto paper plates, "I always knew the big quake was coming, but I have to admit, I was still surprised when it finally happened. It scared the tar out of me."

Reesa nodded in agreement as she distributed the food to the visitors.

While Gary finished off his third serving of beans, Flint described the hours of industrious work that he had done following the disaster. "I checked on your place. The power and water are out. Everything inside is topsy-turvy. I couldn't find any obvious structural damage but you would know better about those sorts of things."

Gary motioned to the old man's house, "What about you?"

"The chimney fell down and killed one of the old geese. Most of the windows are broken. The big china hutch tipped over in the dining room. All of Reesa's prized teacups were lost. There's busted porcelain everywhere," he shook his head sadly. "With the aftershocks and all of the mess inside, we decided to sleep outside tonight."

"That's not a bad idea."

Later in the flickery firelight, Reesa carefully inspected Kayla's swollen arm. "Your daddy needs to get this checked out by a doctor, darling." The old woman looked up at Gary, "Tomorrow, if at all possible."

The man nodded.

After Cat exchanged the black rain boots for a clean pair of Reesa's white socks and pink slippers, she sat patiently on a lawn chair while Gwen helped Flint clean up her scabby forehead wound. The little girl watched with great interest as she held a red plastic flashlight for the old man.

Flint stopped his work and turned to the little girl, "What do you think, doc?"

"Bangs," Gwen smirked. "She needs bangs."

Cat chuckled. "Or maybe a nice hat."

Flint set aside the damp hand towel. "Well; you'll have one heck of a scar, but the actual gash is not too bad."

Gary yawned, "I've got to get some sleep soon."

"With the water being out and the toilets not working," Reesa mentioned, "we put together a little outhouse behind the garage. Does anyone need to use it before you leave?"

Cat and Gwen nodded and Flint led them away with the flashlight.

When the group disappeared behind the corner of the darkened garage, Kayla turned to Reesa. "I'm really worried about Gwen. I think she's going to be really sad about her brother's death and her missing parents." She stared imploringly at the old woman, "Could we borrow a kitten for awhile to keep her company?"

"Ah;" a grandmotherly smile lit Reesa's face, "leave it to me."

Gary kissed his daughter's dusty brow, "I'm impressed by your altruism, young lady."

The group eventually returned from the makeshift toilet.

Reesa turned to the little girl, "With all of the commotion today, our mama cat has run off and left her babies behind."

Gwen listened with great concern.

"We'll need to pitch in and tend to the helpless little ones for awhile," Reesa said solemnly. "Would you like to take care of one of the kittens for a few days, dear?"

"Yes I would," the child replied wholeheartedly.

Kayla, Gwen and Reesa spent twenty minutes in the dark garage sorting through a plastic clothesbasket filled with eight anxious young cats. Gwen settled on an especially curious gray male tabby. She bundled the fluffy little rascal in an old towel and the kitten favored her with a pleasant purr.

"He's so cute!" Gwen nuzzled the tiny striped face.

Flint joined them. "Your daddy and Miss Torres took the truck over to the house, Kayla. I told him that I'd send you two home with a flashlight when you finished up."

A rumbly little aftershock prompted the group out of the dark building. Kayla wearily clutched the borrowed flashlight and walked the short distance home with the feline laden little girl.

With the headlights from the idling pickup serving as an improvised spotlight, the two girls watched Gary and Cat struggle to drag an unwieldy sofa bed through the front door.

Gwen tilted her head, "Can you hold my baby tiger for a minute?"

"I'll try," the teenager fumbled with the swaddled kitten. "What are you going to do?"

"Help." The girl scurried to the door to aid the overburdened adults.

The motley threesome hauled the cumbersome couch to the far edge of the front lawn, well away from the house. Cat slumped down on the faded blue cushions.

Gary stood with Gwen and admired the laborious accomplishment, "Thanks for the help."

The girl studied the peculiar placement of the furniture, "Why did we take it outside?"

The man smiled at the shrewd question, "I'm worried about things falling on us if there are more aftershocks. So we're sleeping outside tonight."

Gwen scrutinized the serrated glass fragments that dangled from the broken front window of the house, "Good idea."

17. Mending the maimed

Kayla wrestled the billowy sheet away from the playful young cat as she struggled to make the bed. The kitten had grown into a mischievous tomcat that they called "Lucky." The feline reluctantly yielded the bed sheet and darted to the high ground of the adjacent dresser. Kayla shuddered after the impromptu tug of war; even after a year, her left arm was still sore and weak.

And it *had* been a year. Today was the first anniversary of the huge earthquake.

Lucky pawed at the framed photographs that covered much of the dresser, sending one tumbling over the edge to the floor.

Kayla shooed him off and retrieved the fallen snapshot.

She loved this particular photo. It belonged to Gwen, but it was really of the whole cobbled together family. They were on the front porch, Gary and Cat posed proudly on either side of her while Gwen stood slightly askew in front of them with a particularly satisfied grin.

Gwen had since reminded them repeatedly that it was the happiest day of her life.

It had been just two days after Kayla's 18th

birthday in August when the family law judge had given her the permanent and sole guardianship of Gwen. The judge had commented that it was an easy decision to make with so many new orphans looking for homes. Later that day, Reesa and Flint had thrown them a big party to celebrate the happy declaration.

It had been a wonderful but rare victory during a very difficult year.

A week and a half after the earthquake, someone found her Uncle Doug's body at the Weld Shop. A few days later, a man from the Longshoreman's Union tracked them down and reported that Gwen's dad had been killed at the Port. They buried the two men and Rowan a few weeks later. Gwen wistfully waited for news of her missing mother. Three months after the disaster, the coroner in Oakland identified Lisa Mills as one of the thousands who had been killed as a result of the terrible earthquake. They endured yet another sad funeral.

Cat and Kayla had sobbed through the whole thing, but Gwen never did cry.

Kayla rubbed her fingers gently over the happy image of the plucky girl in the photo. In the year that Kayla had known Gwen, the girl had never wept.

She was a tough little survivor.

On the Back of the Beast

Cat Torres had stayed with them the whole time.
For the foreseeable future, the woman had
abandoned any thought of rebuilding her
destroyed house. Cat and her Dad were business
partners now. They called their company
Hendley and Torres Reconstruction and they
were both really busy rebuilding damaged
homes. Reesa told Kayla once with a twinkle in
her eyes that she was betting with Flint that the
two would eventually marry. But for now, they
shared the faded blue sofa bed that had replaced
her Dad's inadequate twin in the recently
refurbished Master Bedroom.

Gwen especially loved Cat and the woman was
often amused by the spirited little girl. The two
of them seemed to see something of themselves
in each other. Kayla smiled to herself; Cat Torres
had become a sort of mother figure for both her
and Gwen.

After the first frightening night huddled together
in the front yard, the four of them had crammed
in the cab of the smashed up old pickup and
drove nearly a hundred miles over treacherous
roads to the Central Valley Medical Center
hospital.

Gwen cheered up the gloomy and sleep-deprived
group by singing funny little camp songs along
the way. She was already becoming the happy
center of their new family.

Cat charmed an Emergency Room doctor into admitting Kayla ahead of many other quake survivors. An Orthopedist performed corrective surgery early the next morning. Occasionally over the past year, when Cat and Kayla squabbled about trivial concerns, her Dad would quietly remind her that the woman had selflessly spent tens of thousands of dollars on the medical bills to repair her arm.

Kayla returned the frame to the dresser next to the dirty and creased photo of Gwen's family that Mrs. Cunningham had found in the rubble of the Second Grade classroom. Gwen had stared silently at the picture of the dead just before bedtime nearly every night for months.

Her Dad watched the sad ritual from the bedroom door one night with her and whispered something about still waters running deep.

Kayla, Cat and Reesa had a long emotional conversation about Gwen late one night on Reesa's back porch. Cat thought that the little girl might believe that her family was not really dead since she had only been told about the deaths by others. Gwen hadn't seen the bodies of her brother and parents. Reesa agreed with Cat, noting that the youngster would have to come to terms with the deaths in her own way.

Lucky followed Kayla from the bedroom to the kitchen. A green post-it note hung from the center of the otherwise bare refrigerator door. *Kayla -- Do your exercises! Love, Gwen* ♥♥♥. She smiled when she thought of Gwen and Cat ganging up on her several times a day to do the dreaded exercises that the Physical Therapist had recently prescribed.

She refilled Lucky's food dish and assembled a sandwich for herself. Her Dad and Flint had fixed the well and damaged plumbing only a few weeks ago. She and Gwen had merrily soaked together in the bathtub for hours to celebrate the return of running water. Kayla carried the meal into the living room and turned on the TV. She poked through the stack of paperwork on the coffee table. Kayla looked over a letter about a life insurance pay out that Gwen was finally going to receive. Someone had apparently stolen her Mom's identity and was trying to collect on the policy from South Carolina. Cat's lawyer had recently straightened everything out for them.

"Our top story today on the Noon News is of course the first anniversary commemoration of the massive earthquake that destroyed much of the San Francisco Bay Area. Let's go to Hector Gonzales live in Oakland..."

Kayla set the letter aside and watched with grim fascination.

A reporter stood next to a dirty yellow backhoe,

"It was at 10:17 AM one year ago today just below this very spot when the Hayward Fault ruptured. The numbers associated with this earthquake are staggering. The 8.9 magnitude quake was the most powerful modern earthquake in the continental U.S. The loss in property damage currently stands at over a hundred and thirty one billion dollars, far higher than any other natural disaster on US soil."

The camera pulled back to reveal a huge bare lot.

"This is the site of the new Epicenter Memorial Park in Oakland, at precisely 10:17 this morning, the Governor dedicated the park to the 47,276 people who died as a result of the colossal earthquake."

While the television showed dignitaries shoving dirt and making speeches, Kayla thought about the many people that she had known who were killed; dozens of high school students and teachers, the school secretary and most of the counseling staff, a few distant neighbors, and especially her Uncle Doug.

"Hector, I understand that the death toll is still rising," the anchorman commented.

"That's right, when crews cleared rubble from this site a few weeks ago, they came upon the badly decomposed body of an elderly shopkeeper named Ida Martinez, who was probably one of the first victims of the earthquake."

"Unbelievable," the TV anchor shook his head slowly. "The President also took note of the somber occasion today. In an Oval Office ceremony, the Chief Executive awarded the Medal of Freedom to twelve people for their exceptional efforts to save the lives of others during the crises. Most notably; Captain Burton Weaver of Alamo who piloted a badly damaged jetliner from San Francisco International to Sacramento saving all 493 on board and to Timothy O'Keefe, Frank Johnson and Thomas James "TJ" O'Keefe for their emergency radio broadcasts that warned thousands of people about the deadly firestorms that followed the earthquake."

• • •

Kayla set down the green vinyl covered dumbbell and wiped the sweat off of her face. It was getting easier to do the exercises, she noted. Lucky's head popped up from the kitty bed in the corner and he soon trotted off to the front door.

The cat nudged expectantly at the door. The knob turned and Gwen clattered into the house, "Did you do your therapy exercises?"

"I just finished, little bossy boots," Kayla grinned proudly. "How was school?"

"Kinda good and kinda sad," Gwen scooped up the purring gray tomcat. "In the morning we had an assembly. The principal dedicated the new classrooms."

"That's great!"

"Next week we get to move out of the trailer and into the new D-Wing."

"What did you do at 10:17?"

"That was the sad part," Gwen sighed. "For 83 seconds we stood quietly and thought about everyone who was lost during the earthquake," a faraway brooding look darkened her face.

"It's OK to be sad about it, Gwen," Kayla reminded her. "I was sad for most of the day when I thought of everyone who died."

The little girl slowly nodded, "I saw Mr. Newman at lunchtime. He told me that there's gonna be a memorial wall at school with everyone's name on it, including Rowan." She snuggled the big cat for a moment.

Lucky twisted around impatiently in the girl's arms before he leapt to the floor.

"After lunch, we wrote a letter to people who died in the earthquake," the little girl pensively said as she watched the cat circle around her feet.

"Do you have the letter with you, little one?" Kayla asked. "I'd love to hear it."

Gwen stroked Lucky's chin for a moment before she nodded.

She unfolded the carefully decorated page and began to read, "Dear Mom, Dad and Rowan, I miss you guys *so* much. Every night I think about you and it makes me sad that you're gone. I'm alright. I live with three great people now. Kayla is eighteen and she's like the perfect big sister. Cat and Gary help Kayla take care of me. I got a crazy kitten from our neighbor Reesa. I named him Lucky because I feel really fortunate to have him. I'm in Mr. Larson's Third Grade class now. During the summer, Cat and I convinced Kayla to take the GED test and she got a High School diploma. We had a HUGE party for her because she studied so hard for it. Now I want her to go to college. You guys were my first family and I will never forget you. Goodbye and love forever, Gwen."

The little girl finished and wiped a thin trail of tears from her cheeks.

"Come here sweetheart." Kayla wrapped her arms protectively around the sobbing child, "It's OK Gwen. It's OK."

About the book:

In 2010, the precariousness of global Plate Tectonics provided me with plenty of material as I wrote *On the Back of the Beast*.

More than sixty earthquakes shook the earth in the first four months of the year. Most were merely moderate, the type that we on the West Coast of the US know well: the ground shudders for a few seconds as if a heavy truck is passing nearby. A few of the earthquakes were monsters: a 7.1 quake in the Solomon Islands that spawned a devastating Tsunami, a massive earthquake in Haiti that killed over 300,000 people, an enormous quake that struck the coast of central Chile killing 525 people and damaged buildings over 400 kilometers away in Santiago, nearly 3,000 were killed in a separate tremor in southern China and 58 died when buildings collapsed during a quake in eastern Turkey.

These were the seismic Beasts of early 2010.

If you don't happen to live in an area that is prone to earthquakes you may not realize that they are fairly common and nearly always quite mild.

When the ground quivers occasionally it is easy for the humans that dwell on it to assume that *all* earthquakes will be minor.

It is that strange sense of communal denial of the omnipresent danger just below that fascinates me.

The 1989 Loma Prieta earthquake rumbled from Santa Cruz through the San Francisco Bay Area knocking down a poorly built section of freeway in Oakland, jiggling loose part of the Bay Bridge and halting the third game of the World Series.

This was our most recent significant earthquake.

I was working as a Building Contractor at the time. I was meeting with a customer in the basement of his house at the base of the Berkeley Hills when the concrete floor below us rippled and the house above us swayed and groaned. We dashed out and watched the light standards undulate in the neighborhood park next door. Within an hour or so everyone knew that scores of people had been killed.

For months afterwards I drove my old white Ford pickup truck to the house at the base of the Berkeley Hills crossing right over the Hayward Fault. I would often wonder why anyone would willingly live *On the Back of the Beast* that would cause huge destruction when it finally awoke.

Twenty-one years later as I wrote the chapter summaries for the book, I decided that the novel would be especially gripping as a collection of personal stories. Starting with the gruesome death of Ida Martinez, each of the otherwise ordinary people in the book faces their own unique pummeling by the seismic monster below their feet.

Disasters show no favorites.

I mercifully decided not to show the grisly deaths of various characters. Fortunately we don't see Ida chopped to bits, Doug drowned in sewage or poor little Rowan crushed by the collapsing Kindergarten classroom. But this sort of slaughter happens in nearly all huge quakes.

Most places mentioned in the book are actual locations in the San Francisco Bay Area; I did change the names of a few well-known landmarks. The site of the radio transmitter is the north peak of Mount Diablo, which towers over my house in the East Bay. "Alviso Hospital" is really the huge Alta Bates Hospital in Berkeley where I was born. I renamed it after Domingo Alviso who was an early Spanish settler in the Bay Area and one of my ancestors. I've long thought that more landmarks should be named after him.

I borrowed from a few especially harrowing accounts of survivors of the September 11th attacks. In particular, some tales of kids who, in the span of a few minutes, lost both parents. Hurricane Katrina supplied me with a frighteningly vivid set of images of the chaos and confusion that follows a disaster. In one news account of the Haitian Earthquake of 2010, an elderly woman dressed in a tattered and dusty bathrobe sat on an Easy chair in the street watching her neighbors franticly dig through the ruins. As the grim work progressed, she held up her hands imploring towards the heavens and begged for mercy.

As for now, I glance around for a quick exit when I enter an old brick building or a liquor store. I generally stay out of basements and I spend as little time as possible in Port-o-potties. *The Beast* is slumbering just below me. Who knows when it will awaken?

S F Chapman, July 2013

If you enjoyed *On the Back of the Beast* by
S F Chapman you might also like the literary fiction
novella *I'm here to help*.

I'm here to help

A NOVEL BY
S F CHAPMAN

It had all seemed so right at the time, Sharon realized with a shudder.

Long ago she had made a collection of tiny and innocent decisions that had precipitated a most profound and unpredictable outcome.

Minutes ago her seventeen-year-old daughter, Renita had stumbled upon the subtle inconsistencies of her birth while completing some college applications. Now she waited reproachfully for Sharon to explain the discrepancies.

It was clearly the time; Sharon brooded uneasily, when she would have to finally disclose to her daughter both the laudable good deeds and the lamentable oversights that had led them to the current situation.

From the files of the Free City Inquisitor's Office:™

The Ripple in Space-Time

S F CHAPMAN

**Book 1 of the *Free City* science fiction adventure series
The Ripple in Space-Time is available from Striped Cat
Press at Amazon.com and fine booksellers worldwide.**

Inspector Ryo Trop of the Free City Inquisitor's
Office is called in when the Lunar Ultra Energy Lab
is destroyed by a mysterious blast.

Ryo quickly discovers that a complex and sinister
scheme is afoot as he searches for clues in the
moldering feudal fiefdoms of the Warlords that
dominate human affairs in 2445.

As he struggles with the difficult case, the same
question keeps popping up: Could the recent wave of
space piracy be connected to the disaster?

Shorts, will be available from Striped Cat Press at
Amazon.com and fine booksellers worldwide in 2014

S F Chapman has produced a great deal of
written work over the past 35 years. *Shorts* is a
collection of some of the best by the talented
author from recent blog postings to decades-old
short stories.

Photographs by the author accompany many of
his tales.

A lifelong Northern Californian, S F Chapman traded his construction job for the more docile profession of novelist in 2008 when the economy faltered.

The tireless author has since written eight books. His first, *I'm here to help* (published by Striped Cat Press in July of 2012), is a literary fiction novella about a teenage daughter looking for answers to some troubling inconsistencies in her birth certificate. *The Ripple in Space-Time* (published by Striped Cat Press in February of 2013) is Chapman's second book. It is an exciting science fiction detective adventure set in a moldering and corrupt future controlled by greedy warlords.

Other completed works awaiting publication are the post-apocalyptic soft science fiction MAC Series consisting of *Floyd 5.136, Xea in the Library* and *Beyond the Habitable Limit*; and a recently completed sequel to *The Ripple in Space-Time* entitled *Torn From On High*.

Chapman is currently writing a rough and tumble literary fiction novel about homelessness called *The Missive In The Margins*.